Great Smoky Mountains Mystery

Great Smoky Mountains Mystery

James R. Fox

ABSOLUTELY AMA*ING eBOOKS

ABSOLUTELY AMAZING eBOOKS

Published by Whiz Bang LLC, 926 Truman Avenue, Key West, Florida 33040, USA.

For information contact:
Publisher@AbsolutelyAmazingEbooks.com

ISBN-13: 978-1945772368 (Absolutely Amazing Ebooks)

ISBN-10: 1945772360

Gracious words are a honeycomb sweet to the soul and healing to the bones

- Proverbs 16:24

Great
Smoky
Mountains
Mystery

Proceed With Caution

The words written in this book might be folklore since there is no documentation to prove it to be factual. Like every tale that has been handed down from one generation to the next, what can be assumed to have happened at times has no validity. The names have been changed to protect the innocent. I leave it up to you; it is all here for the taken. All that I know is what was given to me. I now pass it along to you. There, you have been warned, and do not divulge what you have read or else.

1

THE GREAT SMOKY MOUNTAINS were formed during the Ice Age. For ten centuries the indigenous natives called it their home. They hunted and fished, set up villages that were constructed from logs and mud. Huts that numbered around fifty which were grouped around a town square which was known as the council house. These villages were comprised into clans: long hair, wild potato, bear, bird paint, deer and wolf. Two chiefs were elected through a democratic process, one chief for war, the other for peace. The women were equal to the men in making decisions that would impact the clan.

Not until the 16th Century when the Spanish arrived upon the continent, the Indians had nothing to fear from the outer limits of their hunting grounds. The Spanish invaders were mapping out new territory's pushing west toward the Mississippi River in search of gold. Once the Spanish departed, it wasn't until the 1760's that the Cherokee first encountered settlers who had no intention to leave. The Cherokee withdrew to the Blue Ridge Mountains.

War and disease which the Cherokee had never experienced was now upon them. It decimated the tribe. The Europeans took up residence at Cades Cove where the Cherokee hunted river otters, elk and bison.

The Cherokee clans respected one another. They traded in game, hides and food to take them through the severe winters where the snowfall was measured in feet not inches. Two young braves, Little Wing and Bear Claw, who are brothers of Chief Oceeannalee of the Guatari tribe, are fishing for trout and big mouth bass. They paddle their birch bark canoe ever so slightly keeping a watchful eye out for any swift movement below the surface of the crystal clear waters. It was a chance encounter that two cultures would meet that fateful morning.

On the far eastern bank of the Little River, conquistadors advance, some on foot while the officers ride on horses. Their silver helmets glimmer in the sunlight. Their swords, in the metal scabbards, clink and clang against the knee-high boots of Spanish leather. The two braves do not comprehend what they are witnessing. Never before has the Indians seen such a sight. Surely these visitors must be messengers of the Great Spirit which High Horse, the tribe's medicine man and shaman, had foretold would one day come for them. In a series of dreams, High Horse had visions that would be considered prophecies. Among the conquistadors led by explorer Juan Pardo is a missionary padre Phillipe Santiago. His purpose is to bring Christianity to the natives of the New World.

Little Wing and Bear Claw paddle toward the men and through sign language they are able to communicate with one another. The braves lead the soldiers to the tribe's town of Joara, where the voluptuous and charismatic Chief Oceeannalee greets them. It doesn't take long before the women of the tribe are having sex with the soldiers.

However, the accommodations soon take a turn for the worse as an epidemic of small pox breaks out among the Guatari. Many die and there is tension between the Indians and the Spanish. Padre Santiago was able to convert some members of the tribe but could not convince Chief Oceeannalee.

Early one morning, the padre is in the bushes defecating, when he hears sounds of laughter. He peers through the branches where Oceeannalee is in the river washing her beautiful body. "My Lord she is so lovely. She is the Cleopatra of the New World," he mutters, aroused by her nakedness.

Oceeannalee hears him in the bushes and quickly covers herself with her hands. "Who is there?" she asks.

The red-faced padre shows himself to her. "Forgive me but your beauty has got the better of me. I fear that I have been tempted by the devil," he replies.

"Turn your eyes away so that I can retrieve my clothes," the Chief demands of him.

Later that night the padre was able to enter the Chief's den where he seduced her. Then, like a thief after coming for what he wanted, quickly departed.

Oceeannalee and Santiago never said a word to anyone. But in a few weeks it was apparent that the Chief was pregnant. This was taboo as High Horse interpreted it as another omen. If the Chief were to have a child, the tribe would not survive.

Oceeannalee has no choice but to leave the village. She set off to Demons Anvil a slab of granite that overlooks the Great Smoky Mountains. There she will take her life with her unborn child. Padre Santiago followed after her, hoping that he could stop her in time. Little Wing and Bear Claw propel their canoe into the stream which flows to the Demons Anvil and becomes a waterfall that drops down to the valley several hundred feet below.

Chief Oceeannalee looks down at the treetops, then she hears Santiago's approaching footsteps. The two braves arrive a few moments later and run to their chief. Padre Santiago pleads with Oceeannalee not to take her life. He will give her two purses filled with golden doubloons if she will reconsider and become his wife.

He grabs for her, trying to save her from herself. The two braves rush to them, but it is too late. The Chief and the Padre fall to their death, the purses left behind on the edge of the ledge.

Little Wing picks them up, unloosens the strings and

drops the coins into his hand. The brothers bury the coins in the cave behind the falls. No longer will the coins come into contact with another member of the tribe. They never reveal what happened to either the Chief or the Padre. The brothers related to the tribal members that by the time they arrived at the Demons Anvil, the trail went cold.

The Spanish eventually departed Joara, heading west. As for the Guataris, they all but disappeared from the Great Smoky Mountains. They are the ancient ancestors of the Cherokee.

2

IT WAS SHORTLY AFTER the American Revolution that a small colony of German immigrants set out from Lancaster, Pennsylvania to settle into the Dutch Bottoms of the Great Smoky Mountains. They were a hardy bunch led by Minister Fallow Crowder along with his wife Fidelity and daughter Mabel.

Fallow is a God-fearing man, tall in stature, possesses a moral compass that has no deviation. No vices are evident. His hands are calloused, working as a farmer plowing the earth with a team of oxen. Fidelity is a woman who would make any man to entertain sinful thoughts by which more than one admirer had to deal with Fallow. His wrath was delivered swiftly at the end of a bullwhip. Mabel is a handful who yearns to run away from the confines of being under Fallow's thumb.

Joining the Crowder's is the family Haggards. Brennon is a doctor by trade along with his ailing wife Bonnie and their young son Cassidy. Unbeknown to the settlers, they are uninvited guests who are trespassing on Cherokee hunting grounds. For centuries these lands along the northern rim of the Great Smokies were the Indians home. So vast and dense are the tall timbers that if a fire was to be lit, the white smoke could not be seen unless one was standing above the treetops on an overhanging ledge. The Great Smokies was not only hunting grounds but also the home to the spirits of the fallen souls who dwell among the timber and rock.

It is late in the day the colors of the leaves are changing to shades of red gold and burnt orange. The red spruce and the Fraser fir are turning getting ready for another harsh winter which soon will be covered by the first heavy snows. The red cheek salamander will somehow find a way to survive until early spring. These majestic trees are remnants of once relics that have withstood the last Ice Age. Riding a pack mule the hind quarters covered in pelts of beaver and fox pans for mining the river for gold, is Duncan Edge. He can only be described as being a bear of a man, wearing a coonskin cap, with a musket strapped over his left shoulder leather pants mule skinner boots a flannel shirt with suspenders across a barrel chest. His hair is chestnut in color long and matted so is the full beard. His hands and face are red and chapped from the weather. Duncan slides off the back of the mule to take a mouthful of water from the creek. In the reflection of the shallow waters as Duncan's hands are cupped to quench his thirst a hunting party of Cherokee have dismounted from their ponies, armed with tomahawks and knifes.

Duncan is without his weapon the long rifle a few feet away and out of reach. There are three braves in the hunting party led by Mohe, nephew of Chief Oconostota. The other two braves, Adahy and Tsiyi, spread out to box in Duncan. Duncan stands up raises his hands to show that he is unarmed and means them no harm.

The braves are dressed in buckskin loincloths, their chests are covered in a vest made from elk bones. In their raven black hair are eagle feathers, Adahy and Tsiyi sport a single feather Mohe has a pair one behind each ear. The braves communicate to one another in the language of the Cherokee.

Duncan reads their body movements that their intentions are to harm him. Duncan points to his pack mule as he slowly takes steps toward the musket. He isn't about to go out without a fight. Adahy makes the first move Duncan grabs a handful of pebbles, then throws them at the braves face. Tsiyi rushes Duncan, the trapper elbows the brave in the ribs takes him down.

Now it is just him and Mohe. Eye-to-eye, the trapper still unarmed the Indian with a tomahawk by his side. When all of a sudden out from the clearing steps Cassidy with his coon dog Flea, who are in pursuit of a jack rabbit. For a fleeting moment Mohe's attention is now fixed on the boy exactly the diversion Duncan desperately needs.

Quickly the musket is cocked and at the ready as he trains the long barrel at Mohe's chest. Tsiyi and Adahy stop dead in their tracks. Cassidy grabs for his slingshot tucked inside the back pocket of the patched britches. Cassidy pulls back on the slingshot a stone is propelled that strikes the nape of Tsiyi stinging him smartly. He winces in pain. Flea scampers toward the encounter barking in defiance, he is fearless.

Duncan pokes the muzzle of the musket into Mohe's chest prodding him to retreat or else suffer the consequences. The Cherokee in haste make their way back into the woods.

"That was mighty brave of you boy, you saved my life."

"Aw shucks, it was nothing I was just following my dog Flea hunting for supper. That jack rabbit caught Flea's attention I reckon."

"It's getting dark, you better run along back to where you come from. I don't trust those redskins never can tell if they are hiding in the woods waiting to scalp us."

"I can't go home until I get me a critter otherwise my pa will fix a whipping on me."

In the thick bush just behind Cassidy there is movement. Duncan raises the musket pulls back on the silver hammer his finger curls around the trigger. "Don't you dare flinch when I say scoot down do it. Ready?"

"Ready." "

Now scoot down!"

Cassidy drops to the ground Duncan squeezes the trigger the hammer ignites the gunpowder -- a flash of light -- then a plume of white smoke from the muzzle of the gun propels a lead ball across the open field. The intended target drops dead in its tracks.

Cassidy turns to see what Duncan was firing at. "Was it the Injuns who circled back to get us?"

Duncan lowers the musket, pats the boy on his head. "Nope better than that," he pushes aside the tall brush and grabs a wild turkey that is fighting to stay alive. He takes the bird by the neck and gives it a quick stiff twist killing the turkey. "Here you go kid, a fresh Turkey for your dinner table."

Cassidy's eyes light up with delight. "Gosh, mister that's mighty nice of you, I really appreciate your kind generosity."

"No, thanks to you, If you didn't show up when you did, them Injuns would have had my scalp by now I reckon, sure as stink from a skunk."

Cassidy whistles for Flea and tosses the dead turkey over his shoulder. "I can't wait to show my folks what I got for dinner. I'll be heading for home now."

"Keep a keen eye out for them Injuns young fella."

"I will. Flea can smell a rabbit that's hiding so a bunch of Injuns is easier to spot, plus I got my trusty slingshot to protect me for sure."

Duncan smiles at Cassidy and keeps watch over him until the boy is out of sight. He straps the musket over his shoulder, grabs the reins, and gives it a tug. The stubborn mule resists, then they head on out following the creek where he will set up camp as soon as the sun starts to set in the western sky.

3

THE AMISH COLONY has established a settlement at the mouth of the Pigeon River where the land is conducive for farming. The homes are firmly built from the solid spruce and fir timber that framed the walls, floors and the roofs. A one-room schoolhouse was completed just in time before the fall harvest. The children attend school six days a week; on the Sabbath the school was used as a church.

Those that followed Fallow Crowder to Dutch Bottoms numbered close to one hundred. There was Meecham, Dorothy, and their children Abigail and David Broom. Meecham is a blacksmith by trade.

There is William Adams, Anne, and their children Hester and Monroe. William is a carpenter who supervised the colony with the construction of the buildings.

There is the tailor, Philip Smart, along with Zoe and their children Elizabeth and Timothy.

Then there is the farmer Arthur Lynch, along with Candice and their children Rebecca and Seth. The children are all teenagers who are friends and have feelings for one another.

The Sabbath Day was the day that Fallow Crowder looked forward to. He would stand at the pulpit to deliver a sermon about fire and brimstone. The entire congregation was riveted in their seats hanging on to his every word.

Seated in the front pew were Mabel and Fidelity. Fallow stares at them as he begins. "There is God the Almighty and there is the Devil, the guardian of hell. The right hand is Heaven, the left hand is Hell."

Fallow raises his arms above his head, then lowers them before his chest, the fingers tightly gripped together.

"The road to perdition is smooth as a baby's bottom while the road to heaven is rutted and rough. Those that take the first road have no idea who will greet them when they arrive at their destination. But there are signposts, warning the traveler, the seven deadly cardinal sins: anger, gluttony, pride, sloth, envy, greed, and lust. There is no going back from where you came. The second road will be a challenge not many will succeed because it is supposed to be difficult. God's only son Jesus walked down the very same road carrying the cross on his bloody shoulders."

"Amen, give praise to Jesus," rings out from the members of the congregation.

Fallow's hands are red as a beet as he applies pressure, his brow is furrowed he raises his head to the wooden rafters. "Judgment Day is coming. Are you ready to face your maker?"

"Amen we are ready," they reply.

"Will you denounce Satan and all of his evil works?"

"We shall, amen."

"Will you give yourself up to our Lord and Savior Jesus?"

"We shall praise him hallelujah."

Fallow unclasps his hands holds them tight by his sides clenched in fists. "Are you ready to fight for your souls against the prince of darkness?"

"We are, minister," someone shouts from the rear of the church.

"If you see a family member or one of our neighbors committing sin, chastise them first, then bring them to me. As the elder and leader of the church I command you to obey me."

"Amen, you are our leader," Fidelity shouts as she stands and claps her hands. "Praise, may it be to Jesus!"

~ ~ ~

Meanwhile, inside the council house of the Cherokee,

Chief Koatohee was listening to the testimony of Mohe Tsiyi and Adahy's encounter with Duncan Edge and Cassidy. Arriving a few minutes tardy is Oconostota, the war chief. He takes his place next to Koatohee sitting cross-legged. The women of the tribe stand with their backs to the walls.

Once the braves have concluded, it is time for the chiefs to address the meeting. "It is good that you returned to us unharmed. The Great Spirit was protecting you from harm." Koatohee looks around those gathered to see if his words have made an impact. Some of the men nod their heads, others remain silent and stoic.

Next to speak is Oconostota. "Chief Koatohee, you are an old man who has been our leader for many moons, who has kept our people safe. But now there are palefaces that have come to our lands and will not leave. If we do not defend ourselves we might as well surrender all that is sacred to us." The men of the tribe shout whoop and holler their pleasure to his words. "What do you want us to do? Keep the peace or declare war?"

"We want war," are the words he wants to hear. The pounding of the tom toms resonate as the chant we want war echo throughout the council house.

Koatohee lowers his eyes then stands to address the gathering. "The tribe has spoken I hope you have made the right decision. Your actions will affect your children and their children's children. I will not be a part of this. I stand back and let Oconostota be in charge, may the Great Spirit defend you in battle against our enemies, from this day and tomorrow."

4

EVERYONE HAS A PAST and Duncan Edge is no exception. There is a well-known establishment in Chicago, near the stockyards where a gentleman can partake in a game of poker and a choice of whores if you are so inclined. The Riverboat Gambler Saloon was the hottest spot east of the Mississippi that attracted all types, if you had the money to ante up a new deck of cards just waiting to be dealt.

Edge was feeling lucky one Friday night. He slid into an unoccupied seat right beside the dealer, a Chinese girl who was easy on the eyes -- you might say, a real looker. Edge orders a whiskey then unbuttons his jacket. Right across from him is Sid Vincent, a house regular who is having a run of bad luck. To Edge's left is Victor Buren a railroad ramrod. To Edge's right is Brad Clifton, a drifter just like himself.

After a few hands have been dealt Vincent bails and takes an exit. Now it's just Edge, Buren and Clifton. A half-hour later Buren has lost all of his chips. So now it is just Clifton and Edge.

The dealer changes the deck for a fresh one glances over to the owner of the house Sky Gatlin, who is standing at the bar chatting up the regulars. Sky removes a thin cigar from his vest pocket, strikes a match on the bar, then saunters over to the poker table to take in the action. Clifton and Edge both have a stack of chips in front of them. They are both feeling lucky. "Evening gents can I freshen up your drinks?" Sky asks them as he puts his hand around the dealer's slender waist.

"Sure why not make mine a double shot of the good stuff," Edge tells him keeping his hand close to the chest.

"I'm good," replies Clifton.

Sky snaps his fingers, then points to the barkeeper who pours the drink for Edge. A waitress switches out the empty shot glass for a taller one filled to the brim, then sets it down in front of Edge. "How about we raise the stakes on the hand you're holding," suggests Sky.

Clifton looks at his hand, then at Edge, then the pot on the table. He removes his hat and wipes his brow with the sleeve of his shirt. "I'm good with that," Clifton tells Sky.

Sky looks to Edge. "How about you mister?"

Edge is holding two pair of aces and fours, a pretty good hand, but with the smile on Clifton's face he can't tell what he might be holding. Edge downs the drink, then turns the glass upside down. "Hey, what the hell, why not? It's only money, right?"

Clifton goes all in, pushes his pile of chips to the center of the table. Edge is $20 short of Clifton's raise. "Will you take a gentleman's agreement to an IOU to cover the bet?" Sky asks Clifton.

"Sure, why not?" Then Clifton drops his cards kings and tens. Edge shakes his head before he shows his winning hand. Then he rakes the winning pot of chips into his hat and pockets. Clifton slumps in his chair a look of shock and dejection.

Edge tosses him a $20 chip. "There you go, I always make good on my debts."

Clifton walks out of the saloon through the swinging doors. Sky and Edge find an empty table in the corner facing the piano player. "So tell me where did you learn to play poker like that?"

"Here and there. I've been hustling most of my life. Why do you want to know?"

"I could use a guy like you to keep an eye on some of the games being played."

"Are you offering me a job?"

"Do you need one?"

"It all depends."

"Depends on what?"

"How much does it pay?" Sky smiles at him.

"Free room and board and let's say a few bits for starters."

"When do you want me to start?"

"How about tomorrow afternoon unless you have other plans."

"Sounds good to me, I'll see you then."

They shake on it, then Edge steps out into the street. Edge passes a dark alley where Clifton lies in wait. He pulls out a twin barrel derringer pokes it into Edge's back. "Don't make any false moves or I'll drop you here like a mangy dog." Edge raises his hands over his head. The street is deserted except for a stray cat chasing after a sewer rat. "I don't know how you did it but you cheated me. Were you and that smooth talker in cahoots?"

"Look mister I never met him or the dealer. If you want what I won you can have it."

Clifton's free hand spins Edge around and in so doing Edge grabs for his gun. They struggle for control. Two shots are fired and Clifton falls to the gutter mortally wounded.

Within seconds a policeman making his rounds blows his whistle then runs to the scene of the crime. Edge drops the gun and takes off with the policeman in hot pursuit. Edge heads toward the stockyards where he is able to find a place to hide in a stall. He drops to the dirt floor just before the policeman dashes past. Edge decides not to press his luck and stays put.

Wanted dead or alive posters are dispersed throughout Chicago that depicts a composite drawing of what Edge looks like in case he should be seen. A bounty hunter who is close friend of Sky's sets out to bring Edge in. Branch Walker, a wrangler and a sharpshooter, is tenacious and hell bent to claim the reward on Edge's capture. Duncan

Edge will head west with the bounty hunter hot on his trail. Sooner or later they will meet; it is just a matter of time and who will live or die, we shall see.

5

A CLUSTER OF DENSE DARK CLOUDS cross over the tall timbers casting shadows across the meadow, river, and open fields that obscure the harvest moon. It is time to set the watch. The elders of the Amish colony will sleep next to their wives as their sons will stand guard. David and Timothy will make the rounds securing the perimeter from a surprise raid from the Indians.

As the last of the lamp oil has been spent the tiny flame flickers no more. In the cloak of darkness, Abagail pushes the covers aside, then slides out of bed, careful to not make a sound. She does not don her shoes as she tiptoes to the front door. Meecham and Dorothy are sound asleep out for the night.

From house to house she travels, tapping ever so lightly on the bedroom windowpanes awaking Hester, Elizabeth, Rebecca, and Mabel to come join her. Once the girls are all together they head straight to the sheds near the barn. They keep out of sight in the dark shadows until David and Timothy are not near.

Mabel opens the closest shed, then descends the wooden steps into the root cellar. It is black as pitch as she gropes the dirt walls to seek what needs to be found. A stack of bottles lined up in a row are filled to the brim with fermenting fruits. Mabel removes several corks then places them into her apron and returns to the girls.

They check to see if the coast is clear, then in single file proceed into the cornfield. Once they are out of sight they form a circle and sit down among the tall stalks.

Cassidy awakens in his bed because Flea has pulled off the covers. "What are you doing Flea? You'll wake everyone up, hush now go back to sleep."

Flea continues to tug on the bedding. Earlier in the day Cassidy caught a bullfrog that has now escaped. "Is that what you're trying to tell me Flea? Come on lets go fetch him, lead the way."

Flea heads straight into the cornfield. The girls have lit a fire and are charring the corks which they will use to darken their faces. "Who shall we conjure up?" Hester asks as the girls hold hands.

"Let's have a séance who shall we try to communicate with?" asks Abagail.

"I know just who to call. He is Beelzebub. He often visits me," replies Rebecca.

"Send us a sign we implore you," said Mabel. A black cat with red eyes circles the girls as they fall under the spell.

With that, Flea and Cassidy come upon the group, attracted by the croaking bullfrog. "Jeremiah, there you are!"

"Yes, we hear you. You have heard our pleas," said Elizabeth excited with delight.

Cassidy grabs for the elusive Jeremiah, then eyes the girls. "What are you doing here in the middle of the night?"

"What are you doing, Cassidy? Spying on us so you can tell the elders?" Abagail replies rebuking him.

"I lost my bullfrog; that's why I'm here. Now I'm heading back before I get a whipping from my pa."

Mabel grabs his arm tightly. "Don't you dare tell anyone about us being here in the cornfield or else!"

Cassidy looks at their faces blackened from the charred cork. "You have my word, now let me go," he says as he tries to get free from Mabel's tight grip.

Off in the distance is the sound of footsteps approaching. It is Seth and Monroe. They have just replaced David and Timothy on the watch.

"What shall we do if they find us? For sure we shall be

severely punished for our actions," Rebecca cries as she cowers in fear.

"Don't you worry I'll take care of it," Cassidy tells her. "Come on Flea we have to go home now." He heads toward the colony the way he came, then walks out of the cornfield where Seth and Monroe are waiting.

"What are you doing outside? Don't you know you could have been killed? We thought you were an Indian," Seth tells him.

Cassidy shows them the bullfrog stuffed inside his britches. The girls' cover has not been compromised. They wait until all is clear, then return to their homes. Their secret is safe for the time being.

~ ~ ~

Doctor Haggard was in charge of not only tending to the medical needs of the colony but to see that the harvested fruits would turn into wine. Down into the root cellar the good doctor steps to find the bottles missing the cork stoppers. He is perplexed. Why would someone come into the root cellar to take only the corks and not the bottles? He shakes his head in dismay then proceeds back up the steps closing the door behind him.

The women are busy cleaning clothes down by the river. It is the only place where they can congregate and the men are not present.

"Do you think the upcoming winter will be a severe one?" Fidelity asks. Bonnie.

"Oh I do hope not. What will we do if our food supply runs low?"

"Fear not for the good Lord will see to it that we shall persevere," Dorothy replies while wringing out the wet clothes.

"Where in tar nation was Hester that her dress smells like smoke?" Anne asks the women.

"Yes mine as well," Zoe replies.

Candice holds Rebecca's garment and it also has the odor of smoke. "All of our daughters have a lot of explaining to do for sure."

"No matter how hard I try I cannot remove these darn stains," Fidelity declares in desperation.

The sons of the elders are out in the woods sawing and chopping down the trees that will be used in the stone fireplaces that will heat their homes. Cassidy sits on a stub of a fir whittling away on a branch. His legs are crossed as he wiggles his toes while Flea sits by his side scratching ticks from his ear.

A topic of conversation arises concerning the young girls fills the air. "Boy, I sure think that Rebecca Lynch would make a fine wife," says Seth as he splits apart a piece of the lumber with an axe.

"Me, I got my eyes set on Hester. She really is mighty fine, yes sir," Monroe replies as he tosses a load of wood into the wagon.

"What about you, Seth? Which gal strikes your fancy?" David asks.

Seth has a hard time putting words together. "I ... don't ... know ... I never ... gave it much of a ... thought."

"Cat got your tongue again," wise cracks Monroe, as he makes fun of Seth's speech impediment.

Timothy pushes Monroe in the chest. "Leave him be or else you'll have to answer to me."

"What about Mabel Crowder? When I grow up I'll be looking for a gal just like her, I reckon. Yes sir she is the one for me," Cassidy proclaims as he points the branch at them.

Monroe lets out a hearty roar. "Well, you better grow up fast because Mabel will be long taken by then."

"Her father is a task master. Any boy that even dares to look at her will be taken to the wood shed," comments David, wiping his sweaty brow.

"Well enough talk about the loves of our hearts. We

need to start concentrating on the task at hand. We haven't much daylight left before the watch is set."

"You're right, David. Boy, I wish I could stand guard against them Injuns. Yup, just me and old Flea, with my trusty slingshot. Did I tell you that I hit an Injun with a stone? Why I wasn't more than a few paces from him, stung him real good, I did. Heck, why I even saved a strangers life, I did."

"Here we go again with another hair-brained tale of yours, Cassidy," says Monroe shaking his head in disbelief.

"Every word I said is true, like it was written in the good book. The stranger then shot a wild turkey and he gave it to me in return for saving his hide." Cassidy snaps his suspenders with his thumbs.

"Did this stranger have a name?" David asks him.

"Nope I never asked him," Cassidy replies.

"And what about the Indians? They all up and died?" David wants to know.

"The stranger poked his rifle into one of the Injuns chest, then all of them went into the woods."

"All of them, Cassidy? There was more than one?" Monroe wants to know.

"There were three, yup, three Injuns. Me and the stranger scared them all real good. Heck, I didn't see hide or hair of them all the way back home."

"Well, from now on don't venture far away from the colony. If you encountered three Indians, there surely must be many more from where they came from," Seth replies as he is able for the first time in his life, able to finish a sentence without pausing after every word.

~ ~ ~

Later that evening, the elders meet at Minister Crowder's to discuss the future plans of the colony. Meecham Broom, William Adams, Philip Smart, and Arthur Lynch have already arrived. Fidelity and Mabel, scurry about, pouring wine into the pewter steins for their guests.

Then the door opens: it is Doctor Haggard. Mabel takes his hat and the overcoat.

"Thank you for your patience. My punctuality has been delayed due to an unexpected death." He lights up his clay pipe, as he finds an empty chair at the table.

"Who was it that passed away? Was it Rose Commons?" asks Mabel.

"No, she will outlive us all, being the age that she be. I never thought she would have survived the arduous trip, but she is tougher than I ever could have imagined." Haggard exhales a white plume of smoke, which lingers over the table. "Then who was it, Doctor? Our curiosity is peaked," Meecham wants to know.

"It was Liam Spivey. He was working in the woods several days ago and as he was clearing the low-lying brush, he felt a sharp stinging pain in the lower right calf, just above the bootstrap. Liam thought nothing of it, then continued to complete the task." Fidelity places a filled pewter stein in front of him. "By the time I was alerted, Liam was running a fever that I could not break. I believe he was bitten by a recluse spider."

"I will start at sunup to build him a coffin," Adams advises the elders.

"Duly noted, William. I will say a few words at his grave. How is the family holding up?"

"As best they can. He left behind five children and a worrisome widow."

"We shall provide for them in every way possible," Philip states, wiping his wet lips with his sleeve.

"Now that we have heard the bad news to one of our members, we need to shore up our defenses around the perimeter of the colony, so that, in case of an unforeseen attack there will be time to take up arms and position our men."

"We must build a fieldstone wall. There are plenty of rocks in the riverbed. We could delay the felling of trees until the wall is done."

"What a brilliant suggestion, Philip. All in favor say aye."

All vote for the suggestion. "Fidelity, the bottle on the table is empty. Mabel, go to the root cellar and fetch us more wine."

"Yes father," she curtseys, then departs. While they are waiting for her to return, the doctor recalls the missing bottle corks. "Have any of you, been to the root cellar recently?"

They remain silent. Then Mabel returns and places the new wine bottle on the table. Fidelity pulls the cork and places it in front of Fallow. He pours the wine.

"Why do you want to know doctor?" Fidelity asks him.

"There were several bottles that were missing the corks. I know for a fact because I sealed them myself. I record and place the label with the date affixed to every bottle."

Mabel steps behind Fidelity, fearful of where this is going to lead. "May I address the doctor's concern, Fallow?"

"By all means, if you have any information that concerns this matter, state your witness for us."

Fidelity looks at their daughter, who hides her face. Fidelity lifts Mabel's chin. "I was at the river this morning, washing our clothes with the women. Is it by chance that your clothes smelled of smoke, my child? Not only yours, but Abagail's, Hester's, Elizabeth's, and Rebecca's. Why is that Mabel, pray tell us?"

Mabel doesn't know what to say.

"Child, have you any knowledge as to the disappearance of the corks? Speak up," demands Fallow.

"No, father, I do not."

"Are you sure?" Fidelity asks her.

"Yes, mother, I do not know who may have taken them."

"Well, we shall get to the bottom of this. We will call the mothers to testify. There shall be a swift judgment, once the facts come to light."

With that, the meeting adjourns and the men depart. But Haggard takes Fallow aside. "We need to snip this before it buds. You know how the Amish are, Fallow. Anything out of place is construed to be the works of the devil. Be prudent, my friend, in whatever may come out of this."

~~ ~

Later that night a raiding party of Cherokee surround the colony led by Oconostota. He divides the braves into two groups. Mohe will lead the attack from the cornfield, while Oconostota shall lead the main war party from the woods.

Fallow is restless, he cannot sleep. He rises from the bed, careful not to wake Fidelity. As a matter of precaution, he takes the flintlock, then opens the door and steps outside. To his surprise, the watch is nowhere to be found. He makes the rounds within the colony. He is incensed that the young men are derelict in their vigilance.

Fallow's instincts kicks in: he senses a foreboding presence. He pulls the rope connected to the schools bell and the sound of the clapper breaks the silent night. "To arms, to arms we are being attacked!"

The Indians initiate the raid regardless of the alert. Into the colony they advance as the men have scant time to react. Fallow raises his weapon, takes aim and fires at an Indian but a few paces near. The brave falls mortally wounded, shot in the head. The fighting intensifies as the war party separates into smaller bands. Fighting becomes hand-to-hand as the marauders break into the homes. The screams of the women and children becomes a crescendo amid the whoops of the war party.

Through the chaos of the carnage, Fallow somehow manages to make it back to his home with little time to spare. "Fidelity, take Mabel, then gather the women and children. Go to the cornfield where you will be safe. Be quick, take the knives and the cleaver. Do not hesitate to use them. I will come for you if the Lord Almighty shall protect us from our enemy." Fallow hugs and kisses them, then watches as they make their way to the barn.

The homes that have been attacked are torched and the colony is swiftly turned into a burning inferno. The men regroup but are forced to take a stand inside the schoolhouse. A few brave men have overturned wagons to be used as cover from the Indians archers. Wave after wave of arrows soar through the air, some hitting the intended targets as cries for help can be heard. The colony is heavily outnumbered. Fidelity along with Mabel manages to make it to the cornfield where Mohe and the rest of the war party await them. Cassidy and Flea hear their cries for help, and runs to their aid. Tsiyi pulls back on his bow, then releases an arrow that just barely misses the boy, but grazes the dog. Flea yelps in pain. Cassidy turns to help his canine companion. Two braves swoop in to grab them.

Fidelity and Mabel are surrounded. They are the only women to have made it from the colony to the cornfield. The incessant war whoops have lessened and so has the gunfire. It doesn't take long until the war party discovers where the women are hiding in the cornfield. Along with Cassidy, they are rounded up. Mohe regroups with Tsiyi as several braves want to take their scalps and kill them.

Mohe intercedes on their behalf. "We have no reason to take their lives. They mean us no harm."

"If we let them live, they will only give birth to more white men that one day will kill our children and their children," Adahy reproofs him.

"Enough, we take them back to our people. There inside

the council house their fate will be decided."

The Cherokee leave the cornfield and make their way back to the camp. There are numerous women and children who were brutally murdered, who less than a few hours ago were safe inside their beds. Among the recently departed are: William and Anne Adams, Elizabeth and Zoe Smart, the Moyer family, and the Detweilers. All were brutally murdered and scalped. Most of the homes were torched.

If not for the brave men taking a stand, all would have been lost. The women who survived the attack had hid in the root cellars at the outcropping of the wooden sheds.

Fallow searches for Fidelity and Mabel in the cornfield with David, Monroe, Timothy, and Seth, where they find the cleaver and the knife. Flea's faint whimpers are heard, that sound bringing them to the dog. Fallow cradles Flea into his arms. The dog licks his face in a gesture of gratitude. Doctor Haggard is able to remove the arrow that almost took the dog's life.

The dead are arranged for burial, husbands with their wives and children. First things first, now is the time for grieving, tomorrow will be the time to exact retribution for what the savages have brought to the colony.

"What have we done that would have God to abandon us," Bonnie Haggard asks Fallow.

"I do not know. It is not up to us to question why." Fallow washes his bloody hands in an oaken bucket then pours it over the remains of what once was his home, now blackened and charred.

~ ~ ~

Duncan Edge rides up, taking off his hat as he wipes his brow with a bandana. It is difficult for him to contemplate the devastation, needless to say from the shock on the faces of the survivors. The aftermath of the battle is apparent to Edge, the walking wounded still dressed in their torn and bloody clothes. Not one member of the colony was left unscathed.

The Cherokee dragged and shouldered the dead and wounded braves before they left Dutch Bottoms. There are still arrows, the remnants to what transpired in the colony.

Edge dismounts and ties up the horse to a wheel of an overturned wagon. He spits out a mouthful of tobacco. Fallow is supervising the young men in resurrecting the frame to a new house. A rope and pulley are hooked up to the back of a wagon. Seth snaps the reins as the team of horses pulls the wooden structure and it is slowly raised. The men set it firmly in place with hammers and ten-penny nails.

"From the looks of things, it would appear that you were paid a visit by a war party." Duncan removes an arrow stuck in the barn's door, paying attention to the shaft and feathers. "Cherokee, for sure. I encountered a scouting party awhile back. If it weren't for a kid, I'd be skewered on a spit, I reckon."

"That would be Cassidy Haggard, stranger," says Fallow, extending his hand to him.

"Duncan Edge, pleased to meet you. Heck, I'm pleased to meet anyone these days. Living out in the woods can make a fella plumb loco."

Brennon Haggard moseys up and introduces himself. "Might you be the stranger that Cassidy told us about?"

Duncan grins as he spits out another mouthful of tobacco. "That's some boy you got. He saved my hide from them Injuns. I sure hope you enjoyed the turkey. Say, where is your son?" He looks past Haggard, hoping to spot Cassidy.

Haggard gets chocked up, then clenches his fist as he bites his lip. "They took him along with my wife and daughter," Fallow tells Edge.

"How long gone are they?"

"Two days ago," replies Haggard. "

So they have at least 20 miles between us; we don't have much time. If you want to see them alive, we need to head on out."

"But who will take care of the colony? We can't leave the women and children unprotected," Arthur Lynch advises Duncan.

"If it were my kin, I'd go through the gates of hell to rescue them from the devil himself. I have a pretty good idea just where they might be holding out."

Fallow rolls down his sleeves, wipes his hands on the front of his pants. "I will be riding with you, Mister Edge. Brennon, you are in charge until I return. We could use some backup. Who will be joining us?"

"They killed my ma and pa, so I'm with you," Monroe tells him.

"Please don't go. We already lost our parents. I don't want to lose my brother as well," Hester pleads with him as she holds his arm.

Fallow and the young men load a wagon filled with provisions that will have to last them as they travel through the rough terrain. They kiss their loved ones farewell, then depart with the wagon following Duncan Edge.

6

THE WAR PARTY AT LAST ARRIVE at their camp. Fidelity, Mabel, and Cassidy are in tow with their wrists tied tightly with strips of rawhide. The women of the camp throw pebbles and use twigs to assault the captives. Fidelity is struck in the cheek, the cut causing a trickle of blood to stream down her face. A pack of dogs, growl and snap at their heels as they are pulled along into the center of the camp.

Chief Koatohee steps out from his lodge. The entire camp is in a frenzy, whooping and hollering, wanting to take action upon their hostages. Mabel is terrified and her dress is now stained with her urine. Fidelity applies pressure to her bloody cheek. Cassidy tries to show the Indians that he is not afraid of them. He is very brave for such a young age.

Chief Oconostota will address the tribe. "It is a good day to be Cherokee. The Great Spirit has led us to victory. We will not sit by as old men and let our land and our way of life be taken from us."

The women and the boy are forced to their knees before the chief. "What do you want the tribe to do with the pale faces?"

"Kill them," respond several women.

Now it is Chief Koatohee's turn to speak. "What have these women and the boy done to deserve death? Have they tried to kill us, have they hunted us like a wounded animal? No, they have not. Why have you brought them to our camp, Oconostota? Haven't you seen enough bloodshed when you took our braves on the path of war?"

"Let them die," Tsiyi shouts to him. "If the white man had attacked the camp, there would not be one Indian standing here today."

"What Tsiyi truly believes inside his heart is also felt by many. What other choice is there but to kill them," Oconostota concurs.

Mohe who is next in line to be chief pushes aside Adahy. "We do not know for certain what path the white men would take against us. True, they have come into our land with no intention of leaving. But they come in peace. I saw with my own eyes how they defended their families from us. I look at what we have done and how far we need to go for us to survive. Do not resort to more bloodshed, better to have left it along the war path than to stain our camp with one drop more."

The camp is divided, but there can only be one final decision. "Take them to the lodge of Wise Sparrow who is blind. There they will be out of sight until a vote can be cast by the council members."

"You are a wise chief, Koatohee," Mohe proudly proclaims.

Fidelity Mabel and Cassidy rise to their feet and are escorted into her lodge.

~ ~ ~

The trail of the Cherokee war party is in an easterly direction that takes the searchers to the foothills of Thunderhead Mountain. There they will set up camp until dawn's early light. The temperature has significantly dropped now that the last days of autumn have past.

Edge tracks off into the woods in search of game. Seth and Timothy set up a campfire to cook as Fallow opens his worn Good Book to find a passage to read for their supper.

Edge, the seasoned trapper, returns with a pair of squirrel and a raccoon draped over his shoulders. "Here you go," as he tosses the critters to Seth. "Skin them, and we'll have us a belly full."

Around the campfire they more or less get acquainted.

Edge tears off a bite with his teeth. "So where you all from," he asks them.

"We left Pennsylvania for a chance to spread the word of the Lord," Fallow responds while picking the bones clean with his greasy hands.

"Looking back, if it weren't for your belief, you all would have been better off staying put."

"The good Lord will provide for us, Mister Edge," Timothy tells the trapper adding his thoughts to the conversation.

"Where are you from," Seth asks Edge.

"Don't rightly know. I never knew my ma or pa. I grew up with an Aunt Josie who was a hard drinker. She didn't know the first thing about rearing a kid. So next thing I know, I'm shipped off to a big old black nanny who has a brood of niglets to care for. But she gave me my first real taste of loving." His eyes fill up with tears and tender thoughts of her.

"But enough about the past. We need to focus on why we are here, rescuing the women and the boy," Fallow tells them.

"The last thing those Injuns will suspect is that you will search for them. That's what we have on our side, the element of surprise."

"We'll get them just like they got us, sleeping unaware," Seth comments as he spits out morsels of food.

Fallow hasn't had the time, or the wherewithal to bridge the topic until now. "Why wasn't the watch set the night we were attacked? Not one of you were on guard. If not for me being restless in bed, all would have been lost. One must be vigilant for the wolf is forever at the door."

Edge unstraps the bedroll from his horse, then clears a spot on the ground. He lays the loaded musket at arm's length.

Fallow has no need to remind the young men who will

be staying awake until the dawn.

~ ~ ~

The hostage's first night inside the lodge of Wise Sparrow was spent conversing in low whispers for they could not sleep. Fear was constantly on their minds. Wise Sparrow overhears Fidelity and Mabel. "I'm so sorry, mother, that all of this is happening to us."

"That's not true, child," Fidelity replies as she holds Mabel to her breast.

"It was I that took the cork stoppers."

Fidelity looks at her surprised by the confession. "Why for what reason did you do that?"

"Do you remember when I was a little girl and Ida Mae, the black slave, would watch me while you saw to grandma?"

"Yes I do child."

"Well Ida Mae would open her paisley traveling bag. Inside it were little black-faced dolls that had pins in them. Then she would remove a cork stopper from a bottle light a match to char the cork. Then she would smear my face with the cork so we looked alike. Ida Mae told me that if I chanted the name of Beelzebub, magic would happen."

Fidelity tightly squeezes Mabel's hand. "So you and the girls partook in this activity? Tell me that it isn't true."

"Yes mother we did."

Wise Sparrow can't help herself for being an eavesdropper.

Once it is sunrise, a group of women enter the lodge with breakfast. The hostages have not eaten since early yesterday; needless to say they are famished. Then Cassidy is taken from the lodge to be housed in a separate lodge just for men. Mabel and Fidelity are then stripped of their garments and washed head to foot by the same group of women. Fidelity has a Caesarian scar on her abdomen from giving birth to Mabel which has the Indian squaws captivated. Wise Sparrow feels the scar as the women converse in Cherokee. Fidelity is then dressed in deerskin.

Now it is Mabel's turn to be examined. They have her lie down on her back on a bison rug. Mabel is a virgin; she has never been with a man. Wise Sparrow dips a piece of soft deer hide into a wooden bowl that is a mixture of wild honey and maple sap. Then Mabel cries out in pain as she is poked and prodded. The squaws apply scented water all over Mabel's body then dress her in deerskin before departing the lodge.

"Are you all right, Mabel?"

"I feel so ashamed, mother. Why did they do that to me?"

"Because now you are a member of the tribe," Wise Sparrow tells her.

Fidelity and Mabel are stunned by her words. "You speak English?" Fidelity asks the blind woman.

"Yes I do, but I haven't spoken it for a very long time. You see, I was just like you. I was captured after my husband was murdered defending our home. I was taken hostage and I thought the Indians would kill me for sure. But for some unexplained reason, my life was spared. I always had poor vision, until one day I went blind."

"What will become of us and little Cassidy? Oh I perish the thought of what those savages have in mind."

Wise Sparrow consoles them. "Don't worry, my dears. The good chief Koatohee considers me to be a visionary that can foresee the future. I will tell him that if they harm you or the boy, the Great Spirit will bring dark clouds across the land. There will be no game to hunt, or fish to catch, no birds to lay eggs. All will perish."

Suddenly there are footsteps just outside the lodge. "Whatever you do, don't tell anyone that I spoke to you in our language," she tells them.

"It will be our secret, Wise Sparrow," Fidelity assures

her.

"Priscilla Darrow is my Christian name; my husband was Bartholomew. We once lived in Quincy, Massachusetts. Oh how I wish we had never left home. We could have grown older together, but alas, now it is too late."

7

THE SEARCHERS ARE BEING observed on high above the treeline. A sudden rush of pebbles slide down on the path they travel. Edge pulls hard on the reins of his mount. "This is as far as we go with the horses," he tells Fallow and the boys.

Fallow ties the reins of the wagon to the handbrake that slows the wheels to a stop.

"From now on our route is upward." All eyes take in the tall timbers and the steep slope that await them.

Edge dismounts and unstraps the saddle from the horse. He removes the bridle and bit, then gives the horse a hard slap. It trots away back down the path. Seth and Timothy unload the supplies from the wagon as Fallow follows the trapper's lead.

Edge surveys the tough terrain that they will have to undertake. He knows how difficult it will be to conquer this trail, especially for the boys and Fallow, who are not familiar with the mountains. Edge points in the direction they will travel. "Keep your eyes peeled for any quick or sudden movement. I'm going to double back, just to be safe. When you get to the higher elevation, you will be able to see a large group of white boulders. Head toward them. When you get there, follow the trees that are notched out belt high. I put them there to help make it easier to climb the mountain terrain. If all goes well, I'll catch up with you." Edge takes off and soon Fallow and the boys are out of sight.

Watching them is the bounty hunter Branch Walker, all the way from Chicago. He has been trailing the group since daylight. Walker's hair is snow-white, covering his shoulders, and he sports a full beard. His spyglass had given away his position to the trapper as it reflected in the late afternoon sun.

Edge knows the territory better than most he has managed to survive a mountain lion attack with only a knife. Edge has built several huts that are well camouflaged. He also has set bear traps that will provide meat and hides to get him through the heavy snows of the unpredictable winters in the mountains.

Up the steep incline, Fallow and the boys advance, clutching at low-lying tree branches while their boots seek a firm foundation to advance to the top of Thunderhead Mountain. As one another reaches out their hands to assist, Seth can't help but wonder why Edge left them. "I have my doubts about Mister Edge."

"Why so, Seth? He seems to be an honorable man," replies Fallow as he holds onto a split rock to keep from falling.

Timothy grabs hold of Seth's outstretched hand as they advance. "I just have a feeling in my gut, that's all. Maybe he's planning to bushwhack us, once we get to the top of this godforsaken mountain. How do we know he's not in cahoots with the Cherokee?"

"Seth, you have a wild imagination. That trapper could have killed us the first night as we slept out under the stars. Why would he want to now do us in," Timothy asks Seth.

"Well we don't have our horses or the wagon and we have just enough supplies strapped on our backs. I've heard tales about folks just like us who were killed for less," comments Seth as he bends over trying to catch his breath.

"The good Lord is watching over us," Fallow tells them.

"A lot of good God did to protect Mabel, Cassidy, and your wife," shouts Seth.

"Don't blame God, Seth. He has no hand in what we do to one another," replies Timothy as he gives him a boost. Fallow grips Seth's hand pulling him up to the top of the boulder.

Between the grunts and heavy breathing, Timothy wonders. "Do you think we will be able to rescue them?"

"For certain we will. I have no doubt in my mind that it will be done."

"Gosh, I wish I had your faith, minister. After what those heathen bloodthirsty savages did to our colony, killing women and children in cold blood, as if they were lambs to the slaughter, there's no telling what they might do to the boy and your women folk."

They have at last reached the cluster of white boulders and just like Edge had told them there were several trees with notches that denoted the trail. "Do you think we should set up camp for the night? From this vantage point, we have a clear view down the mountain and these boulders can provide us protection. Come sunup we can set out on the marked trail."

"You make it hard not to agree with you, Timothy. Yes, let us rest here for the time being. Seth, fetch us some wood to start a fire, while I'll fix us something to eat. Timothy, venture not too far and see if you can find us some water to quench our thirst."

~ ~ ~

Inside the great council lodge there is a gathering of the chiefs and the braves who are loyal to them. Chief Koatohee and Mohe sit on the bearskin rugs, Chief Oconostota and Adahy sit on a buffalo hide. "Now is the time to vote on what to do with our captives. Do we let them live among us or do we put them to death?" Oconostota asks the members.

Voices are raised for and against the proposal.

"Tsiyi, go to Wise Sparrow's lodge and bring her and the captives so we can decide their fate."

Tsiyi obeys the chief while the peace pipe is passed around the lodge. Tsiyi soon returns with Wise Sparrow, Fidelity, Mabel, and Cassidy. Their attire resembles the rest of the tribe. The women's hair, are in braids that drape down their backs. Cassidy is wearing a deerskin loincloth.

"Wise Sparrow, have you anything to say that will sway us to vote for or against our enemies," Koatohee asks.

Wise Sparrow is assisted by Mohe to the center of the lodge. "Many moons ago I stood before a tribal meeting that was to decide my fate. I know now, having lived among the Cherokee for so long that you respect your elders in regard to what they have to say. Although I no longer can see your faces, I know that to kill innocent women and children are not what should be done. You are proud Cherokee. I have lost my husband, who like myself was born white. That was the design of the Great Spirit. He has created everything, from the night sky to the deepest waters, to the top of the mountains to the lowest meadows. The women are mother and daughter; one gave life, the other will do the same. The boy will grow to be a man, a brave if you let him. They mean you no harm. If you allow them to live, then the Great Spirit will be pleased. If you decide that they should die, then there will be grave consequences which will befall the tribe. I had a dream where many more whites will arrive but they will not be here to farm or to hunt. No they will come to take you away, put you in chains. You will not have a choice for a treaty to be signed granting peace. But it is not up to me, it is all in your hands."

~ ~ ~

Darkness falls and the air is cool and crisp. Edge, who is familiar with the trails of the mountains, knows that whoever is stalking them is now the one being sought. Edge and Walker are survivalists who are tenacious and will not stop until they get their man.

Edge arrives at one of the hidden huts, then checks out the bear traps that were set several weeks ago. Inside the hut is a cache of gunpowder, iron balls for the musket, also pelts of raccoon, jackrabbits, and squirrel to keep him warm.

Edge positions himself into the snug hut, then waits. It doesn't take long before he hears movement in the brush close by. The trapper pulls back the hammer of the gun, anticipates anything that might be outside. It is a large black bear; Edge can hear the grunts as it moves closer to the hut. Then the bear steps into a trap. The bear's left leg is caught as the spring snaps, closing the metal vise into a tight grip. The bear attempts in vain to pry the leg free. It growls in agony. Back and forth it struggles as blood flows from the wounds.

Edge pops his head out from the hut, then raises the musket and fires off a round which strikes the bear in the head. The bear drops to the ground dead. The sound of the shooting echoes throughout the tall timbers, where Fallow and the boys are camped. The shot is muffled, but they still hear it in the distance.

But the gap between the trapper and the bounty hunter is all the more closer. Walker raises his head from the bedroll and looks east to where the shot was fired. Walker wastes no time as he grabs for his flintlock, then heads east mindful that whoever is out there is armed and dangerous. He must proceed with the utmost caution. One false move could cost him his life.

Fallow picks up his rifle and takes a peek around the boulders. "I'm going to see who fired the shot. You boys stay put until I get back."

"How will we know that it is you? What if we hear footsteps approaching? It might be the Indians, it might be the trapper, or it might be you. It's hard to tell out in these woods in a pitch-black night."

"I'll call out as a dove, so you'll know it's me, Seth."

"You be real careful, minister."

Fallow pats the boys on their shoulders. "Thanks, Timothy. Stay vigilant until I return."

Just as a precaution Edge plunges his knife into the bear's chest. Then he undoes the trap removes the bloody leg. There are deep and jagged puncture wounds that the carnivore sustained. Edge pulls out the knife just as Branch Walker arrives.

"No false moves or I'll shoot you dead."

Edge has his back to the bounty hunter.

"Drop whatever you got, then raise your hands high where I can see them." Walker steps closer to Edge, his rifle pointed at his back. "That's good enough. Now slowly stand up and face me."

About that time is when the good minister shows up. He stays out of sight and watches. He is within earshot of the men. "If you came for the bear, take it. There's plenty more on this mountain for me to kill."

"I didn't come all this way for a measly old bear. You're what I'm after."

"Not I, stranger. You sure you don't have me mistaken for someone else? I never have seen your face before in these here parts."

Walker opens the top button of his long coat as he firmly holds the rifle. He pulls out a wanted poster folded in half. "Here, look at this and tell me what you see."

Edge unfolds the poster which states *WANTED DEAD OR ALIVE. Be on the lookout for this man who killed Brad Clifton.*

The sketch of the killer shares a striking resemblance to Edge. "What are you trying to tell me, stranger? You think I'm this fella who is wanted by the law?"

"Indeed, you were in Chicago and shot this man in cold blood just to watch him die."

"I was never in Chicago. Hell, I never been east of the Ohio River. Sorry, mister, but you're badly mistaken. It isn't me you're looking for."

"Oh I got my man and I intend to take you back where

you will stand trial for this killing of an innocent man."

Fallow has heard enough he can see where this incident is headed for. "Drop your weapon where you stand or I'll see to it that you get a proper send off, by golly."

The bounty hunter isn't about to relinquish the gun. "That's not going to happen. This man is coming with me."

For a split second, Walker turns his attention away from Edge to face Fallow. Edge grabs for Walker's rifle, then they fight over it for control. Fallow rifle-butts Walker upside his skull and the bounty hunter's knees buckle from the powerful blow.

Edge takes the rifle, then aims it at Walker. Blood starts to trickle into his ear. "I'm beholden to you, Crowder. You plum saved my hide for sure."

Walker holds his throbbing head. "You're making a big mistake taking up with the likes of a scallywag who is wanted by the law."

"What you are claiming about Mister Edge may or may not be true, I have no way of knowing. But what I do know about him is that he's helping me find my family and a boy who were taken by the Cherokee. Now what kind of a man who has no stake in my affairs sees fit to help me, unless he is a good man, a God fearing man with moral principles? Can you tell me that, stranger?"

Walker is speechless as he wipes his bloody hand on the coat. "Suppose you are right, and I'm wrong about him. Now I'm not saying yes or no, but this here wanted poster sure looks a lot like him." He hands it to Fallow. "Surely you would have to agree."

Fallow glances at the poster, then at Edge. "Heck, the fella on the paper has no beard, the eyes are close together, not like my friend."

"Well, it was dark when the killing happened; it was over real fast. The only one that saw what happened was a constable making his rounds. He gave chase but the killer gave the lawman the slip."

"Well then, there you go. I'm in the clear, stranger. I reckon you been looking in the wrong place. Maybe this fella you're after never left the city. Maybe he's holding up somewhere having a good old time right now, I bet." Edge has a big grin on his face as he cuts through the carcass of the bear.

Walker feels like such a fool, that all of his tracking has been all for naught. "I can't go back there, not empty handed anyways. I'd be the laughing stock of Chicago. My reputation will be shot through, like a can of beans used for target practice sitting on a fence."

"We can always use another hand, that is if you want to help," Fallow asks him as he lowers his rifle.

"I did see signs of a possible trail. There was fresh footprints that could have been made by a barefoot boy."

"You don't say, stranger? Where about?" Fallow asks him.

"The names Walker, Branch Walker. The trail was heading north, about a mile back yonder, on the mountain. It was fairly fresh, I reckon."

"That's great news, Walker. Say, why don't I cut up this here bear while it is still fresh, then cook us up some juicy steaks? Then we'll use the bearskin to keep us warm."

"Sounds like a plan to me, Mister Edge. I'll get the boys to join us. Now don't you two tussle anymore until I get back you, hear me?"

Walker and Edge grin back at Fallow. "We'll be fine, now go scoot. Hurry back or else the bear steaks will be gone."

The bounty hunter and the trapper proceed to skin the bear.

8

IT WAS BY THE SLIMMEST of margin that the lives of Mabel, Cassidy, and Fidelity were spared. If not for the testimony of Wise Sparrow, all would have been lost. They would become members of the tribe, but first they would have to go through the indoctrination. The women would have to field-dress a deer. The entire hide would be removed from the carcass. It takes a skilled hand to be able to accomplish the feat. The women were allowed two chances.

Fidelity does it on the first attempt. She had an experienced teacher back home; her brother Ethan was a hunter. Mabel was skittish at first, but she persevered and completed the challenge on the second go round. Cassidy had quite a different path to take in order to be accepted by the Cherokee. A group of young braves take Cassidy into the woods to hunt and fish. Using their bows and arrows, they show Cassidy how to take aim and hit the targets. To the braves' surprise, little Cassidy is very accurate. All of those days using his slingshot had paid off extremely well.

They are awarded new names: Wild Honey for Mabel, Swift Deer for Fidelity, and Sure Shot for Cassidy. From this moment on they would not have to worry about what a new day will hold for them. In many ways, the Amish and the Cherokee lead parallel lives. They deeply care for the family and the land, worship and revere their god. They want their ideals to prosper and flourish so they can be passed down to future generations yet to come.

The Cherokee were never threatened until the Spanish arrived, then it was the English, and now the settlers who are content to call their land home. With each passing day,

Fidelity, Mabel, and Cassidy are slowly adapting to the tribe. They are assigned a task, be it cooking, sewing, tending to the children, caring for the elders, hunting and fishing. If any member of the tribe does not do their fair share, they are severely punished.

Mohe has taken a liking to Wild Honey (Mabel) and she has noticed the brave's attention. The unwed women of the tribe are not pleased with the way the lovers interact. Swift Deer (Fidelity) tells her daughter to stay clear of Mohe's advances. "We may dress and look like the Cherokee, but never forget where we come from."

"I know, mother, but my heart beats for him. I cannot explain my feelings. Can this be love?"

"Has Satan taken up residence inside you? Cast the evil thoughts out of your mind and be not tempted by sins of the flesh."

"I have done nothing wrong to warrant your wrath."

"If only your father was with us at this instance to set you on the moral path to save you from yourself." Their thoughts turn to what may have happened not only to Fallow but the rest of the colony. "Do you remember the last words he spoke to us, I will come for you?"

"Yes, mother, indeed I do. Knowing how determined father is, there will be hell to pay for what the Cherokee have done to our friends and neighbors."

"Exactly that is why you must chase those demons who are trying to pollute your senses with sinful thoughts of the Indian brave. You are young and beautiful; one day you shall take an honorable gentleman to be your husband. Until that day, we can only pray that the good Lord will look after us and keep us safe." They hold each others hands and recite The Lord's Prayer.

9

THE SEARCHERS HAVE ARRIVED at the summit of Thunderhead Mountain. To the east is Cades Cove, north is Meigs Falls, and to the east is the Little River. It is a great expanse of wilderness; the Cherokee camp could be situated anywhere. It will be a Herculean task to determine what trail to follow.

The winds are swiftly blowing in a northeasterly direction as snow begins to fall, quickly covering the top of the mountain. The searchers will have to hunker down and wait out the approaching fast-forming snow swells before they can descend. With just the clothes they are wearing to protect them from the weather, it would have been fatal. But thanks to Edge who killed the black bear, the thick fur provides protection. A makeshift shelter is hastily built from the tall timbers. Their extremities, the tips of the toes and fingers begin to tingle as the early stages of frostbite takes effect. They huddle around the fire to keep warm, for if any member of the search party should succumb to the bitter cold it will greatly affect their plans to rescue the women and the boy. Would they resort to leave one behind to continue on, or to travel back to the colony and get help? Either way, the odds are stacked against them.

Duncan Edge has been in this situation before, same with Branch Walker. They are seasoned veterans who have managed to get out of many a tight jam. But Fallow and the boys have spent most of their lives living comfy and cozy. Frostbite can turn into gangrene that will slow down the blood to the affected area. Any time wasted will ultimately result in death.

The searchers hair and beards are coated in the snow

as the morning sun slowly rises above the tall timbers, spreading daylight over the landscape. They have survived the frozen night on top of Thunderhead Mountain. Seth and Timothy stretch their cramped legs, then they cut down low-lying tree limbs to replace the campfire's dying embers.

Edge prepares the breakfast while Fallow sharpens the blade of his knife. Walker chops away the ice from his rifle and wipes the barrel dry with his bandana. Now that it is daybreak, they have to make it down the mountain to the valley below. It will take most of the morning to navigate the steepest leg of the descent. They must be careful where they step, for the boulders and tress are covered with a thick coating of frost.

Black bears aren't the only carnivores that inhabit the territory in search of food to fill an empty stomach. A female puma has been nursing her newborn litter of cubs, inside a lair during the night. Now she sets out hunting for prey to bring back. With any luck, she will find a raccoon or fox to satisfy her.

In single file, the searchers trek down the steep mountain. Edge is leading at point, followed by Fallow, Walker, Timothy, and Seth who is last. The puma spots their movement off to the right of the lair. Stealthily, she waits as the group advances. The puma's sense of smell is heightened as she ever so slowly closes in for the kill. The butterscotch-colored fur blends in with the winter's foliage. The long tail sways side to side then bobs up and down. The light-colored eyes are locked in on them. One-by-one they pass the big cat now crouched low on an overhanging ledge. She lets out a low growl deep inside the lungs passing through razor sharp fangs. Then the puma leaps from the perch, the claws spread apart. nothing but the mountain air above and below the big cat. Seth is the puma's target as his back takes the brunt of the full impact. The claws dig in deep to Seth's shoulders, knocking him forcefully to the ground.

The big cat wastes no time as the deadly jaws lock fast to Seth's neck. Timothy turns to help, quickly followed by the men. Walker and Edge fire their rifles at close range. The bullets hit the puma in the head and chest, dropping the man-eater dead in its tracks. The cat's large green eyes with jet-black pupils stare back at them.

Fallow and Timothy use all of their strength to roll away the puma from Seth. The boy has deep wounds to his face, neck, and back. He coughs up blood, which is black as he slips into unconsciousness. Fallow grabs Seth as he desperately attempts to keep him alive. But, to no avail. Seth's eyes close then the body becomes limp. He dies in Fallow's arms, gasping a last dying breath.

Fallow's eyes well up with tears he is filled with grief for Seth. He holds him for a brief moment, then lies Seth's body down. They dig a hole in the ground to bury Seth. Fallow opens his worn Bible leafs through the pages until he locates an appropriate passage of scripture to read. *"The righteous perish, and no one ponders it in his heart, devout men are taken away, and no one understands that the righteous are taken away to be spared from evil. Those who walk uprightly enter into peace: they find rest as they lie in death." Isaiah chapter 57, verses 1 and 2.*

They bury him and mark the grave with a makeshift cross.

Timothy is inconsolable because the boys were close as brothers. Now he will keep Seth's memories alive as the searchers continue on the path to locate the camp of the Cherokee. "He was a good friend I'll miss him a heap."

"I know you will, but God has him now."

"All you preachers are the same. If you haven't got an answer to a question, just mention God and all is forgiven," Edge spews as they proceed to hike down the steep terrain. They slip and slide over the still frozen land, staying alert for any sign of a Cherokee hunting party.

"Hey, preacher," calls Walker.

"Yes, is there something on your mind?"

"I'm not a religious man, never much to reading the Good Book, but seems to me the land is covered with crosses over so many graves. Take that kid we just buried up yonder." Walker grabs hold of a pine tree branch then steps on a large flat stone. He then turns around looking up at them. "I get that someone had to make us; what I don't get is why."

Fallow takes his hand, "We do not question the Lord's work; that is left up to him. In good time we'll all get to meet our Maker and one day then and only then, will we fully understand His grand design."

Edge is now next to Walker. "How about what happened to your family, who do you blame?"

"The Indians, Mister Edge, that's who," Timothy tells him. "If it weren't for them, my best friend would still be alive, instead of being put in a hole on this mountain. Nobody will ever get to visit him to pay their respects, to plant fresh flowers and say a few prayers."

Fallow pats the boy's shoulder as they take a rest on the trail. "The last words that he said to me was in faint whispers: 'See to it that you get them back home safe and sound. Promise me so that my life wasn't all in vain.' For sure, Seth, I will."

"Maybe if we were born as Indians instead of white, our opinions would differ," Edge states as he stretches his aching bones.

"You've been living off the land for days at a spell. Don't you ever cross their path?" Walker asks him.

Edge shoots him a glaring look. "So now I'm off the hook for the killing?" Edge spits at Walker's boots.

"You killed somebody, Mister Edge?" inquires Timothy.

Fallow fills the boy in. "I thought the incident was

settled a ways back between you, why bring it up again?"

"Some things are never finished, like a murder that goes unsolved," Walker responds.

"All of us are born with demons and angels that stay with us right up to the very end. Sometimes we control them and then there are times when we are weak."

"Have you ever been tempted, preacher? Have you ever been lost so much that you made a grave mistake that haunts you?" the young man asks.

Fallow furrows his brow, clenches his fists, tightens his jaw, rocks back and forth as the rage deep inside still boils after all these years. "I carry a cross, a heavy cross for what I have done. No man's soul is unblemished and I am no exception."

"Times a-wasting. We have to get a move on if we are to find them alive," Edge tells them. "Let's move on out and burn us some daylight while we can."

10

FOR THE TIME BEING, while a new lodge is being finished, Wild Honey and Swift Deer are bunking with Wise Sparrow. She is teaching them the Cherokee language in order to make it easier to get along with the tribe.

"You are a wise old woman being able to live so long as an outsider and now highly respected among the Indians."

She smiles at the words of Swift Deer that are spoken to her in English. "I am but one voice. You have your daughter who will one day take a brave."

"No, that shall not bear fruit, for my husband will come for our daughter and me. In my heart and soul, God will see to it that we will be reunited."

Wise Sparrow takes her hand. "Does your husband, my dear, command the army? For that is what it will take to fight the Cherokee. Do you not see how many braves there are inside the camp? The Indians will not surrender. They will resist until the last brave has died."

Wild Honey enters the lodge carrying a willow basket filled with fish that Mohe has caught in the river. "We have more than enough fish to last us, mother, thanks to Mohe."

"Did I not tell you more than once to stay away from him? He has lust in his heart that consumes him." She takes the basket of fish from her daughter and tosses it outside the lodge. "I'd rather starve to death, than to take one bite of his catch."

Wild Honey becomes enraged by her mother's cruel act. "Father provided for us, but where is he now, dear mother? Who will take care of us in his absence?"

Swift Deer grabs Wild Honey by the wrist and pulls her to where Wise Sparrow is standing. "Who took care of her?

No one and yet here she stands a survivor, who although she has lost her sight can perceive what you are too blind to see. For every day that we can stay together is one less day before father will arrive to take us back home."

Meanwhile, Sure Shot has adjusted rather well. He enjoys living off the land and has picked up several basic words in Cherokee to help him communicate with members of the tribe. He plies his wood carving skills to craft a new slingshot and is teaching the young braves how to use it to take down small game.

Chief Oconostota has taken a shine to him, Tsiyi is not pleased. He is jealous of the boy and plans to do him harm.

Early one morning, Tsiyi takes Sure Shot into the woods under the pretext that Oconostota will soon arrive to join them. Sure Shot is excited so off they depart. Tsiyi has set a trap for the boy that will put him in harm's way. But no matter how hard Tsiyi tries, Sure Shot will not take the bait. By concentrating all of his efforts to lure the boy, he hasn't noticed that there is a predator nearby.

A wild hog with razor sharp tusks rushes through the dense brush and in its path is Tsiyi. Sure Shot wastes no time as he moves in between the brave and the beast. The boy pulls back on his slingshot and takes aim. The projectile delivers a direct hit right in the snout, but it has no affect.

Tsiyi spins around and grabs Sure Shot with not a moment to spare. The razorback snorts and grunts slows down, then doubles back. The boy and the brave split up, then raise their weapons at the enraged swine. The wild hog is brought down by Tsiyi's well-placed arrow.

Speaking in Cherokee, he tells the boy how if not for his heroics, he would surely have been killed by the wild animal. The brave rests his foot on the wild hogs head as he removes the arrow. He then tucks it back inside the leather quiver strapped over his shoulder. He pats the boy's head, then return back to camp. Any thoughts of jealousy toward

Sure Shot have been removed, and from this day forward Sure Shot will be highly respected. The Cherokee realizes that the boy acted bravely when he could have just stood and watched the wild hog severely gore him.

Tsiyi binds the animal's legs, then places it on his broad shoulders. Later that evening, there is a celebration in the camp. It is rare to have a feast to honor not only a young brave, but one who is not one of their own. The sound of drums fill the air as the men and women dance in separate circles in front of Oconostota and Koatohee. Seated between them is Sure Shot, in recognition for his brave deed.

Tisyi addresses the tribe and describes the encounter with the wild hog. Listening attentively is Wild Honey and Swift Deer. A group of young girls attach a braided leather band around the boy's head and two white eagle feathers which denote his new status among the tribe.

Koatohee presents to him a decorated tomahawk, a gift for being brave. "We are all grateful that you took it upon yourself to defend Tsiyi against a ferocious predator. Your swift decision proves how fearless you were. Tsiti is fortunate to have had you on his side otherwise we would be mourning his death."

Oconostota hands Sure Shot a hunting knife of which the handle is crafted from the bone of an elk. "I am not surprised that Sure Shot knew what had to be done. He is brave beyond his years."

Sure Shot looks at Wild Honey and Swift Deer who are with the other women of the camp. His thoughts drift to his parents. He wonders how they would feel knowing that their only son was being honored by their enemy, the Cherokee. This isn't right. I should not be accepting their appreciation. Instead I must find a way to escape with the women. We have to find a way so that we are able to devise a ruse, so that we can run away.

As the celebration continues into the night, the boy makes his way to the lodge of the blind woman, Wise Sparrow. He is careful not to make a sound as he enters crawling under the buffalo hide that covers the entrance. "Wake up, do not make a sound," he tells the women. "We haven't much time before day breaks. We need to leave right now while there is a slimmer of hope."

"Cassidy, what are you saying? You aren't making any sense. You want us to escape, to where?"

"Into the woods. I know of a place where we can hide out until the men from the colony come. Hurry, gather your belongings."

Wise Sparrow hears what is being said. "Go with the boy. I will stall the braves when they come looking for you".

"Thank you, Priscilla. You are a true friend. We will not forget you." Fidelity hugs her tightly.

"And you as well, Fidelity. May you be safe."

They slip out of the lodge and stay hidden by the shadows until they are close enough to the woods to make a mad dash to freedom. But first they have to ford the river. There are many shallow and deep spots that must be reckoned with. One false step will lead to their capture and possibly death.

They are mid-river when Mohe enters the blind woman's lodge. "Where are the women," he asks.

"They are with the boy. You must have just missed them."

Mohe departs: she listens to his footsteps. "I hope they have made it safely into the woods. Bartholomew, my love, do watch over them, I pray."

Mohe searches the lodge where Sure Shot is dwelling, but there is no sign of him. He then alerts Tsiyi and Adahy. Mohe demands to know who was watching the boy and the women. They have no idea. "We have to find them or the chiefs will have our scalps," Mohe tells them.

The braves quickly arrange a hunting party to take out after them. Mohe heads straight for the river where he finds fresh footprints. He signals to the braves to follow him across the waters. Once they arrive on the outer bank, the trail has gone cold.

"Sure Shot has covered their tracks," surmises Adahy as he tosses the branches used aside.

~ ~ ~

Thanks to Wise Sparrow, the escapees have widened the gap into the wilderness. Cassidy, Mabel, and Fidelity must somehow find a way to elude being captured. They head south in the direction of Thunderhead Mountain. But for the present they are in the valley where there is no place to hide.

Edge is the first to spot them in the far distance, a stirring in the tall grass. He pokes Walker in the ribs then he points to the target. Walker peers through the long glass to where Edge has directed him. The objects are out of focus, so he cannot tell if it is the Cherokee or maybe a herd of deer grazing on the grass.

"Should we send Timothy to scout, just to make sure," Walker asks Fallow.

"Sure, I'll go," Timothy tells them.

"Keep your distance and stay low. When you get close enough to see who or what it may be, wave your hat high in the air."

"Yes sir, Mister Edge, I'll do it for Seth."

Walker watches Timothy through the long glass, then relays to Edge and Fallow what is happening. Timothy closes the gap between them when suddenly the hunting party arrives in the distance. Fallow is the first to spot them. He grabs the long glass from Walker and scans the valley to locate the hunting party. Then he moves his attention to the area where Timothy is hunkered down. "There's Indians heading this way. We have to alert Timothy before it is too late."

Cassidy hears the advancing Cherokee, then crouches low to the ground. "We have to find a place to hide before they see us," he tells Fidelity and Mabel. Timothy is now in view. The women wave and shouts to him. A flock of peregrine falcons take flight, likewise the deer scurry for safety, sensing the ominous danger that awaits them. Timothy runs to Cassidy and the women to embrace. He waves his hat over his head to signal that all is okay. Little does he know but he just gave away their location to the hunting party.

The Cherokee pick up the pace; Cassidy urges they do the same. The hunting party waste no time closing the gap, their whoops and hollers can be heard in the tall grass. Edge, Fallow and Walker raise their rifles and take aim ready to fire if the Cherokee get into striking distance. Mabel and Fidelity are running side-by-side, followed by Cassidy and Timothy. Several braves take aim with their bows and arrows to which Fallow yells "fire." The men pull the triggers, the gun smoke momentarily shrouding their faces. One of the braves is hit and falls down as the arrows are released narrowly missing the intended targets.

"Reload," Walker yells. "Come on, they are gaining on you! "

Edge shouts to them.

Up the rise they scoot to where the men are, the Cherokee right behind them in hot pursuit. "Fire," Fallow calls out as another volley is delivered. Now is not an occasion for a long-time no-see reunion. That will have to wait while they hold off the hunting party.

"Take the women and the boy to higher ground, Timothy, while we make a stand," Fallow commands him.

Fidelity holds on to her husband for dear life. "I won't leave you; I'd rather die next to you than to die alone as an old widow."

Fallow, removes her caress. "Do as I say, woman. Now is not the time to debate. Take our daughter and the boy to shelter. Do not disobey your husband," he sternly stares at her.

With tears in her eyes she turns away, then follows Timothy along with Cassidy and Mabel to the wooded hills.

"We must stop them here," Edge comments as he reloads the flintlock.

"Don't allow them to take the left flank," Walker snaps as he points.

Adahy with a few braves attacking full on are mowed down in a hail of bullets. Tsiyi rushes toward the rise as the men reload their rifles. The Cherokee advance until they are within striking distance. Walker grabs his black powder pistols already cocked and loaded, then fires point blank. Two more braves bite the dust.

Tsiyi attacks Edge with a tomahawk. Edge raises his arm to deflect the blow that strikes his head. They tumble to the ground and wrestle, with Edge holding fast to Tsiyi's forearm. Fallow fires off another round which barely hits Mohe. The men are outnumbered against the Cherokee. Timothy rushes down to assist, firing his musket and then grabbing for the knife tucked into his boot. Walker comes to Edge's aid, his rifle butting Tsiyi in his neck. The Indian drops the tomahawk. Edge seizes it and then smashes the Indians face. The cheekbone cracks from the impact. The men have suddenly turned the tide. They now have the hunting party on the run. They will not be defeated -- no, not today.

Bloody and bruised, the men watch the Cherokee retreat. Mohe helps Tsiyi to his feet, his face is a bloody mess. Mohe raises his arm over his head, telling the braves, "We will return. The white devils may have beaten us for now, but they will soon find out how brave the Cherokee are in battle." They retreat helping the wounded and carrying off the dead.

There is little time to bind wounds as the men, women, and the boy's head back to the colony. The weather has changed from being clear as the winds intensify, now thick and heavy clouds covering the sky. It begins to snow, the fast approaching storm covering the land with a blanket of white.

"There is no way we will be able to reach the colony in this weather," Fallow tells them while holding on to his hat.

"We must head for Rocky Top at once. I know of a safe place where we can get out of the weather and stay dry," Cassidy assures them. Unaware that they are being followed by Mohe and Adahy, they make their way up the wooded slippery slope. Edge falls back to take up the rear, just in case they are being trailed. They arrive just before sundown at Rocky Top where the Demons Anvil is awash with the fast surging icy chunks of the falls.

Edge's instincts are right on point as he spots the Cherokee. He picks up a large rock and hurls it close enough to where the Cherokee are. They stop and hunch down, then proceed with caution. Edge picks up another rock and throws it in the opposite direction. Now the Cherokee think they are surrounded. They look all around, not knowing what to do.

Edge aims his rifle at a tree branch directly above their heads, then discharges his weapon. Pieces of the bark rain down on them as they take for cover.

Walker hears the gunshot, spins around, and heads toward where the shot was fired.

Fallow watches Walker as he runs to help Edge. "The Lord has graced us with Mister Walker and Mister Edge to protect us from our enemies who wish to do us harm. As it is stated in the Bible, Moses was with the Israelites lost in desert, the Lord will rescue us from our oppressors."

Mabel wraps her arms around him. Fallow is unmoved

by his daughters affection. Fidelity looks sternly at her husband. "Have you no love in your heart, Fallow? Can you not see that she longs to be loved by her father? Do you want to know what happened to her? Her virginity was taken from her, not by an act of love, but from a sadistic Indian ritual. Now no gentleman will want her, for she is an impure woman in possession of damage goods."

Mabel looks into her father's eyes that are distant and cold, as a dead man walking among the living. She turns away devastated. "It is my fault that all of this has happened. I am sorry father I have done the unfathomable, invoking the dark one to be present in my life."

Another rifle shot breaks the tension. Timothy is all set to help. "You're needed here," says Fallow. "They will be all right fighting side-by-side. Now we must find a safe place in case the Cherokee come for us."

Cassidy scales the rock formation at the falls as the snowstorm intensifies. Just below Demons Anvil, the boy spots the cave behind the falls. Cassidy enters the cave but it is dark, his vision impaired as he cautiously proceeds. His left foot steps upon a round object, then he loses his balance and falls on a pile of bones that break from his weight. There is a strong stench of death as he brushes himself off and stands.

Cassidy leaves the cave and waves his arms to get the group's attention. "Come, I have found a place for us," he shouts through the swirling snow.

They slowly ascend the rocks in single file. "You are a lifesaver," Fidelity tells him as they hug one another and enter the cave.

"We must start a fire to keep us warm and dry. Try to find something we can use for kindling," Fallow directs them.

Among the many bones are worn and torn pieces of animal hides and clothing. Mabel tugs on what seems to be soft to the touch. She keeps pulling and then the strong stench of decaying flesh fills her nose mouth and lungs. She lets out a strong cough, then turns her head and covers her face with her arm.

Timothy steps outside as he hears the crunching of snow due to oncoming footsteps. It is Walker and Edge helping one another at the foot of the falls. Timothy signals to them. Walker falls to his knees, there is an arrow protruding from his chest. He is in a lot of pain, his breathing hard and labored. From the corner of his mouth a trickle of blood streams down his chapped lips onto his frosty beard.

Edge drapes his right arm around Walker's shoulder while toting the rifles. Timothy makes his way down to help them. By the time they arrive at the entrance to the cave, there is a fire inside that awaits them. Tall shadows flicker on the stone walls, outlines of the living as well as those of skulls and bones; the remains of an ancient civilization.

Edge lowers Walker to the cold, hard ground while Fidelity and Mabel do their best to clean the wound. The arrow must be removed if Walker is to live to see another day. Cassidy fills his hat with water from the falls then Fidelity creases the brim while Mabel raises Walker's head so he can take a drink.

Walker's eyes focus on the ceiling of the cave, which is covered with scenes that depict animals and humans. Walker does all that he can to raise his hand and point to the ceiling. Everyone looks at the depictions. Even though crude in design, the paintings are not difficult to decipher. One of the scenes shows a fort defended by soldiers being attacked by Indians.

"So the legend is real after all," Walker remarks as he lays down his head, then coughs up blood.

"Don't try to speak; you'll only aggravate the wound," Fidelity tells him as she wipes his forehead.

Edge takes Fallow aside so that Walker can't hear them. "He's not going to make it unless we put some grub into his belly. What say I go scout around and see if I can bag us something to eat?"

"Yes that would be prudent. Why not take one of the boys with you?"

"Nope, I'll be all right. Besides, you can never tell if those Injuns might come back. Me and old Walker sure put a scare into them. They hightailed it pronto. He's a good man, make darn sure that you can fix him back to the way he was."

When Edge sets out the winds are howling something fierce, a complete whiteout as darkness falls. The snowdrifts are knee-deep, but Edge has been through storms before. He trudges a few hundred feet when he notices a stirring among the tall timbers. He wipes away the accumulated flakes from his eyelids, then he patiently waits. It is a group of deer, two fawns, a doe, and one large buck. Raising his weapon to take aim, he lets the fawns and the doe move on, the buck his intended target. He has to compensate for the velocity of the wind in order for the bullet to travel the distance where it will bring down the buck in its tracks. The trapper knows that he will only have one shot, for if he misses the group will scatter into the wind.

The buck watches over the deer before it proceeds into the clearing. Through the deep-packed snow, the deer advance. Edge makes sure he is downwind so the deer cannot pick up his smell and be spooked. He is covered head-to-toe like a snowman, every breath exhaling a vapor of steam that covers his face. The buck shakes its head to dislodge the coating of snow from the antlers. The fawns wiggle their ears, the doe picks up her head and looks straight at Edge as he pulls back on the rifle's hammer. The buck turns toward the doe, the exact movement Edge was waiting for. He pulls the trigger and the black powder ignites into a white flash of smoke. The bullet travels across the open field in the blink of an eye, stopping the buck in its tracks. The buck takes two steps, then drops dead as the deer take off back into the woods.

Later, as they sit around the warm fire inside the cave, Cassidy marvels about how Edge brought down the buck during the blizzard. "How did you do that, Mister Edge? I bet there aren't many hunters who could have done what you did."

Edge bites off a chunk of the meat. "The secret is to keep the gunpowder dry. If not, the gun won't fire. Hell, I knew a fella who had his rifle blown to bits, took out his eye, it did."

~ ~ ~

The heavy snows not only affected them, but the Cherokee and the colonists.

The Cherokee performed the death ceremony in which the dead were raised up on a platform made from animal hides. Then a fire was lit underneath the body and it was cremated. They also tended to the wounded who survived the battle. The Indians will have to wait until the weather breaks, then take up the trail to track them down.

The colonists on the other hand will rebuild the fieldstone wall and once completed, it will fortify the perimeter of the entire colony. It has been weeks since Fallow set out with the boys, hence it is assumed that they were killed or were captured by the Cherokee.

If not for Edge being an experienced trapper, familiar with the rugged terrain, they would never have survived. Walker pulls through, once the arrow was removed. It was a tough go, but the bounty hunter held on.

It was early in the morning when Timothy, who was standing guard, heard a pack of dogs barking. There off in the distance was a team of mutts, pulling a sled across the frozen terrain. Snapping a bullwhip is David Broom standing on the wooden runners of the sled, while comfortably seated under a pile of hides is Monroe Adams. "Mush, you mangy dogs," David commands as the team churn up the densely packed snow.

Timothy rushes to them as he falls into a snowdrift. "Hey over here, we've been waiting for you!"

David pulled on the reins, which alerts the team's leader to change direction. David and Monroe help Timothy gain his footing. "Aren't you a sight for sore eyes? Are you all alone out in this wilderness," Monroe asks.

"No, there are the others. Come, follow me to a cave behind the frozen falls." It was just dumb luck that Timothy was at the right spot when he heard the dogs barking.

"It is so good to see you boys. How are the rest of the colony doing?" Fidelity asks them.

"Well, we started rebuilding what was lost. When you did not return after a spell, myself and Monroe got anxious, so we took off on our own." David looks around but doesn't see Seth. "So where's Seth? Boy, I do miss him. I bet he was glad to see you, Mabel, safe and sound."

Fallow tells them the bad news of how he was killed by the mountain lion. "He was a good boy we gave him a proper Christian burial."

They gather up their belongings and set off, the women wrapped up in the hides of the sled. Monroe whistles, signaling the dog team to push off. It will take a few days of travel before they arrive back at the colony.

Edge's trapper instincts have him on the alert as they plod on through the ice and snow. He catches a faint glimpse of movement among the trees that causes him concern. "I have been living on my own for a spell, come across a few bears and mountain lions but it was always a fair fight, one-on-one. But there is one predator that gives me the heebie-jeebies."

"And what might that be, Mister Edge?" Fidelity asks

him.

"The wolf. Now that is a crafty animal, for sure. And why is that you might ask? Well, I'll tell you why. You see, a wolf hunts with a pack, although not all wolves. Some are called lobo, or a lone wolf. But for the most they hunt in packs. There is a leader of the pack and that is the one you have to pay close attention to. If you can manage to take him out, the rest of the pack will scatter."

Edge has a reason to be concerned for his fellow travelers because a wolf pack has been tracking them for the last mile. "We have company and they aren't the Injuns," Edge tells them as he points to the woods off to the north.

"What should we do," Monroe asks him as he guides the dog sled.

"Slow and steady, son, slow and steady. You don't want to spook the dogs, not just yet."

The wolves pick up the pace because it has been a few days since they have had anything to eat. The lead dogs stumble over a rock buried in the snow, causing the rest of the team to slow down to a stop. Edge wipes off his rifle, then tells the men to do the same. The wolf pack has spread out among the trees, waiting for the leader to make the first advancing step.

"We need to make a stand where we are. Women, I would advise you to take cover behind the sled. It might get ugly real soon."

Monroe and David hold fast to the reins of the dogs, for now they can sense the wolves. The dogs bark in reply to the growling of the wolves. And then the predators come out from the woods running like the wind, swift and steady. The pack have a well devised plan of attack: some will go after the dogs while the others will take to the men, women, and boys.

"Shoot to kill, not to wound. It's everyone for himself," shouts Walker as he takes aim with his rifle. The dogs are attacked and fight for their lives. Monroe and David use their knives in defense. The wolves go after the boys. Fallow fires a shot that kills the wolf that has David's arm in its grasp. The dogs put up a valiant fight but are no match against a pack of killers. While the wolves feast on the carcass of the dead dogs, the rest of the pack set their sights on the defenders. Shot after shot are fired, the rifles reloaded and then it resorts to whatever means necessary to stay alive. The sharp knives come out from boots and belts to stave off the tenacity of the wolves.

When all was said and done, five wolves were killed along with all of the dogs, but there were no fatalities. They survived what could have been an undocumented tragedy.

The sled is taken apart and used to build a fire. The remains of the dogs are then cremated as Fallow contemplates on what might have been. "By the grace of God we have been spared to live another day. Our loyal companions did the best they could but were no match against a formidable foe."

~ ~ ~

At long last they arrive back at the colony. Later that day, a celebration is held in their honor. Seth's parents and his sister take the news of his untimely death very hard, but never the less they attend the festivities to give thanks.

Fallow addresses the gathering. "Now I know how Jesus must have felt when he was in the desert for forty days and forty nights. I did not know where my wife and daughter were when I set off to rescue them. Brennon and Bonnie Haggard share with me the loss of their son, Cassidy. I tried not to think of what the Indians would do to them. Instead, I asked the Lord to give me strength, that we could ultimately rescue them. Thanks to Duncan Edge, who is an excellent trapper and guide, we could never have known their whereabouts. And to Branch Walker, what a Godsend you were, sir, indeed. We shall always remember when you decided to help us in our pursuit and may the good Lord protect us against our enemies from this day on."

Several of the people reply, "Amen, Minister Crowder, amen."

Everyday life returns back to the way it was as a new church and stable are built. It is time for Walker and Edge to saddle up and leave. The bounty hunter still has a killer at large who has a price on his head and the trapper yearns to return to his remote refuge. Walker heads east as Edge heads north.

Candice Lynch, Dorothy Broom, Bonnie Haggard are having a quilting bee inside the Crowder's residence to assist Fidelity in readjusting to being Amish. The women sew square-shaped colored patches into a pattern that when completed will be a hexagon, a six-sided star to ward off evil spirits.

The topic of conversation turns to how Fidelity, Mabel, and Cassidy were able to cope as prisoners of the Cherokee. Fidelity is seated by the kitchen window, in her lap is a bowl filled with freshly picked snow peas. She sorts them by size, pleased to be home, among civilized folk. "I don't know if I could have survived. I still have nightmares, seeing our neighbors killed at the hands of those savages."

Mabel enters the home, as Dorothy continues. "Who do they think they are, taking advantage of us? My God, all we ever want is to live in peace."

Mabel joins Fidelity with the sorting. "And so do the Indians as well. No disrespect Mrs. Broom, but we were treated fairly well ..." Mabel's words trails off as she recalls how the Cherokee squaw took from her, her virginity. Mabel lowers her head.

Fidelity consoles her. "If not for Cassidy, we would never would have escaped. He is brave beyond his years."

Bonnie smiles at her. "That he is, Brennon and I made sure of it."

Mabel's presence of mind returns from reflections of the past. "Yes, he saved the day. Oh how I do hope that Wise Sparrow was not blamed for our escape."

"Who is this woman," Candice wants to know more.

Fidelity relates the narrative of how she was taken captive after her husband lost his life from the Indians, then losing her sight and becoming a respected elder among the tribe.

The guests depart, then mother and daughter prepare the evening supper.

Later that night, Fallow is burning the midnight oil. He is inside the church, writing his thoughts down on a piece of parchment with a quill's tip dipped with indigo ink. A plank in the floor creaks near the threshold. Fallow's eyes squint as he sits in the front pew of the church.

"We had a deal, Preacher Crowder. Why are you recanting on your word?" Out from the shadows steps Ida Mae dressed all in gray.

"And what deal do you speak of?"

She takes two steps forward. The black slave looks all around, then glares at him. "This church. You defy me by building another, after the devil himself made his presence known in Lancaster. Is that what you want to happen here at Dutch Bottom's, another church burned down to the ground?"

Fallow throws down the quill. "I should have left you behind, instead of having pity for you. Who is going to take in a slave who has leprosy, tell me, Ida Mae? No one but a God-fearing man like me who leads his flock preaching from the Holy Bible"

The slave reaches into her quilted bag, her hands covered with threadbare mittens, and takes out a small black-faced doll made from pieces of cloths sewn together. Tucked inside her bonnet are hatpins, which she removes one by one. Then she sticks the pins into the doll's arms and legs. Fallow senses great pain in his limbs. "This is just the beginning for there will be more to follow if you defy me." She then tucks the doll back into the bag and leaves the church.

Fallow is gripped in fear his body is soaking wet from perspiration as the candles flame dies out.

11

WHEN THEY WERE INSIDE the cave at Demons Anvil the scenes depicted on the ceiling has left a mental image, not only to Branch Walker, but Duncan Edge as well. Surely the depiction of the fort all ablaze, the Indians and the soldiers in battle, must have occurred nearby.

Rumors have spread about how the Spanish conquistadors left behind a lost buried treasure of gold. The whereabouts are unknown. The sole survivor of the Spanish garrison at Fort San Juan was never seen again. Could his remains be part of those in the cave at Demons Anvil? Could he have made a deal with the Indians to spare his life in return for the gold? The Great Smoky Mountains is so vast it would take a prospector, years to search all of the hidden caves and still come up empty handed.

If the Cherokee had the gold, then Fidelity, Mabel, or Cassidy would have seen it when they were held captive. Wise Sparrow never mentioned a word about gold or the Spanish to them; therefore the mystery remains.

In the center of the church cemetery is an old hickory tree. Cassidy's dog is busy digging at a hole worn away by erosion. "What have you got there, Flea? Is it a squirrel, or maybe a pesky chipmunk? Move over, let me see what's got your attention."

The dog barks as Cassidy drops to his knees beside the tree. He places his arm inside the hole in the tree. The fingertips touch an object that is round and soft. Cassidy tugs on it and gingerly pulls it out. The dog wags its tail, his ears straight up, tongue hanging down, as he waits. The boy rubs off the layers of dirt that has accumulated from being inside the tree. It is a leather pouch bound and waxed with a red seal.

Watching his every move is Ida Mae. Creeping up, she startles him. "What have you got there, boy? Let me see it," she lays a hand on his shoulder.

Cassidy jumps back, holding the pouch tightly to his chest.

"Don't you know that you shouldn't go poking around where you don't belong? The cemetery is filled with lost souls, ghosts just waiting to snatch up little children and take them away to a bad place."

Flea growls at her and that alerts the boy's mother. "Cassidy, it's time for supper," Bonnie calls to him. The boy and his dog sprint for home, but not before Ida Mae gets in the last words. "I got my eye on you, boy, you hear? We're not finished with what you found. If it belongs to the dead, then it's mine."

At the dinner table, Cassidy shows his parents what he found. Brennon dons his spectacles. "The intricate seal tells me that what the pouch contains is an official document."

"Really, Pa, who do you think it belongs to?"

"Hard to say, son. Let's break the seal and we'll soon find out."

"Okay, Pa, open it."

Bonnie has a suggestion. "Brennon my dear, since Cassidy discovered it, don't you think he should be the one to do the honors?"

"Right you are, Bonnie, by all means. Cassidy unwrap the mystery. After all these years of being hidden, you will be the first to know."

Bonnie wipes her hands on the apron as she removes the dinnerware from the table. The seal is broken, then the flap is folded over. Inside the pouch is a letter written in Spanish. "What does it say, Pa? Can you translate it?"

"Being a physician, I had to learn Latin, so from what I can gather it is from the year 1568, addressed to the Queen

of Spain, requesting additional soldiers to defend Fort San
Juan from the Indians. The letter goes on to state that a
shipment of gold will be moved to safeguard it in case the
fort should be overtaken. It is signed by Juan Pardo, affixed
with the official red wax seal."

Cassidy snaps his fingers, his eyes wide open filled with
surprise. "When we were hiding out from the Injuns inside
a cave, there was a drawing on the ceiling that showed a fort
being attacked. Could it be the same one that the letter
mentions, Pa?"

Bonnie sweeps the floor while Flea eats the crumbs
from the supper.

"Where did you find this?"

"In the cemetery, Pa. It was inside a hole in the big
tree."

"I see. Well, if the letter and the description of what you
saw in the cave are one in the same, then maybe the gold is
buried in these here parts. "

"It's time for bed, wash up. Before you know it, the sun
will rise up on a new day."

"Yes, Ma." Cassidy kisses them goodnight.

~ ~ ~

Ever since the colony was attacked by the Cherokee, the
evening watch has added extra sentries as a precaution. The
young men are instructed what steps are needed to be taken
in a call to arms. The Amish believe in non-violence.

Fallow has had his faith questioned. How could this
have happened, not only to the colonists, but to his wife and
daughter? God tested Job to no end, so now in a roundabout
way it is Fallow's turn in a test of faith under fire.

When Fallow was a little boy, his father constantly beat
him and his mother. It all came to an end when a millstone
crushed his father's head, stopping the day-in day-out
abuse. Fallow was just eleven and had to take care of his
siblings and their mother. She began to drink and in so

doing took it out on his sisters. They found her body at the bottom of a well.

That is when he found God and began to understand his station in life. He married Fidelity and then they had a daughter who they named Mabel. Fallow was ordained and became a minister. He was assigned to a small community in Lancaster, where the Amish welcomed him warmly.

Again, darkness found him, as rumors spread regarding witches performing a black mass. Fallow would have none of it, dismissing it because there was no definitive proof. That is when the church was engulfed in flames. The congregation believed it was the work of the devil and threatened to kill him and his family. Reluctantly, Fallow had no choice so he acquiesced with a small group of loyal neighbors to set out for the Great Smoky Mountains.

Once they arrived, the livestock became a constant challenge to protect from an unsuspected predator. Many a chicken, piglet or lamb was snatched and taken off into the woods. It was better to lose a few than to risk a life in pursuit of a hungry animal.

~ ~ ~

The winter took its toll on the Cherokee as their food supply became low, so hunting parties were sent out from their camp. A band of Cherokee raided the colony in the dead of night. The watch was alerted as several men chased the braves into the woods where they were ambushed. All but one was killed and scalped; he barely made it back alive.

"Will we ever live in peace," Candice asks her husband Arthur as she tends to the gravely wounded man.

"As long as there are Indians, we'll never be able to hang up our guns."

Cassidy made darn sure to stay clear of Ida Mae, now that he knows what the letter contains. If anybody is going to find the lost gold, it will be his and his alone.

Ida Mae has the power of persuasion in her quilted bag of tricks. She has a peculiar talent that is hard to resist. It all began with an innocent invitation, nothing more than a subtle suggestion. The young women who are unmarried would pluck wild berries that will be used for jams or fermented to make wine. Those that were bitter to the taste will be used for dyes to color wool and cotton. The unwed ladies wear blue bonnets to signify their status within the colony.

One day, while doing the laundry at the water's edge, Rebecca has just picked red berries, transferring the juices onto a white bonnet and staining it a deep crimson. The color will not dissolve no matter how hard she tries. The color is vibrant compared to the soiled clothes. Rebecca turns over the large wicker basket, then spreads the wet red bonnet to dry in the noonday sun.

Ida Mae has been watching her. "Why don't you try it on? It will frame your pretty face, Miss Lynch."

Rebecca smiles at the black woman. "I couldn't, I dare not, what would the elders say to such a bold act?"

Ida Mae smirks at her words. "A red bonnet is just a hat to cover your hair, nothing more."

"Oh no, not in the eyes of the Amish, red is the devils favorite color," Rebecca replies, as she dries her hands on the apron.

Ida Mae brushes away a few strands of Rebecca's hair from her face. Rebecca recoils from the moldy woolen mitten that covers the leper's hand.

"And if I were the devil's advocate, I would state that God created all, including the most beautiful flower, the red rose. But to pluck one, you must be careful not to be pricked by the thorns."

Their conversation attracts Mabel, Hester, and Abagail, who surround them, laden down with baskets full of wet wash. Abagail picks up the red bonnet, which is now dry, trying it on, tying the strings into a bow under her chin.

"The color is to die for. We all must have one for our own," surmises Hester.

"Yes, you should. Cast away the blue bonnets for the red. They are bolder and will make a statement instead of being told what to wear by the elders. You can send a message that a change has come to Dutch Bottoms."

They blush and Mabel is absolutely stunned by the black woman's words, for it is sure to bring retribution by the men of the colony, especially her father, Minister Crowder. So for the time being, the red bonnet will be hidden away, but where?

Ida Mae decides to take it shortly after it was left behind. Inside her quarters, she gathers bolts of white cloth, then using a pair of scissors she busies herself in fabricating bonnets, one for each of the fair maidens. It is a difficult task, for her hands are brittle from the leprosy. Taking a spool of thread, she has all to do to ply the end through the eye of the needle. She is consumed with a scheme that will test all who perceive her as an outcast. She is someone to accuse, the scapegoat whenever something bad happens and there is no rhyme or reason why. Ida Mae will have her way by manipulating those most precious, full of promise and hope. What better scheme can there be than to persuade the maidens that what they truly believe can no longer remain hidden? It is time to stir the ever simmering cauldron with new ingredients of a secret recipe. Once she gains their trust with the gifts of the red bonnets, her powers will be unstoppable.

12

MABEL IS HAVING A HARD TIME sleeping as her mind wanders back to when she was held captive. She longs to see Mohe once again. She wonders if he feels the same about her. What could have been, if had they not decided to escape? Perhaps their lives would have been for the better, but now all she can do is dream.

Wise Sparrow hears a stirring inside her lodge and she is fearful. "Who is there," she asks.

A firm hand touches her. "It is I, Mohe. Do not be afraid, for I mean you no harm."

"Why are you here? Is it still not the night?"

"Yes, how do you know that if you cannot see?"

She sits up in her bed and with his help she gets to her feet to stand. "When I lost my sight, my sense of hearing became more attuned so that what I cannot see, I can still remember."

Mohe guides her to the buffalo hides which cover the dirt floor, together they sit facing one another. "So tell me what is on your mind? Could it be Wild Honey, the young woman that you fancy?"

He smiles at her. "You truly are wise for an old woman. I do have feelings for her, but now she is with her family and I am left to hunger."

"Why not tell her how you feel for her in a letter?"

He looks at her with puzzlement. "What is a letter, Wise Sparrow?"

"You take the words that you speak and place them on a piece of parchment in order that they can be read."

"But I do not know how. I have never been taught to read or write."

The old woman smiles at him, then she strokes his hands. "If you bring to me a smooth hide and juices from the berries, I could write the letter for you."

And so that is exactly what Mohe does. Wise Sparrow composes a letter to Wild Honey. She dips the tip of her pinkie into the dark juice then places it on the hide in alphabetical letters, and when she is done she gives it to him.

Mohe approaches the colony early the next morning when he encounters Cassidy with Flea. The Indian grabs the boy around his waist and covers his mouth so he cannot scream. Flea barks at Mohe, so the Indian kicks the dog ever so gently, hoping to keep him quiet. Cassidy kicks his legs as he tries to get free from Mohe's grip. The Indian lowers the boy to the ground and then shows him the knife threatening him if he makes a sound. Cassidy obeys, then pats Flea's head to assure the dog that everything is all right.

In sign language, Mohe instructs Cassidy that he wants the letter to be delivered to Wild Honey. The boy nods his head, then Mohe leaves him.

Cassidy waits until the opportune time to give Mabel his letter. They are alone where no one else can see them. Mabel reads the heartfelt letter which makes her cry.

"He does have feelings for me. Oh what should I do, Cassidy?"

"He's an Injun and you're not. You belong here with your family, just like he belongs with his tribe. Are you willing to risk it all, Mabel?"

She gives him a peck on his cheek. "You are so wise, smarter than I. Yes, it is true for it could never be. I will have to reply to Mohe and let him know it can never be possible."

13

THE FIRST AMISH CHURCH in Switzerland split from the Anabaptists in 1693. There they were persecuted for their beliefs, thrown into prisons, often times never to be seen again. Once they departed Europe, they settled in Pennsylvania, particularly Lancaster County, Lehigh and Bethlehem. The region was ideal for farming which suited most of the Amish.

The church services were officiated by a bishop or minister, depending on the size of the congregation. The men and women would be seated in separate sections, the service would last approximately three hours. Hymns would be sung from the Ausburd, which were full of sorrow, loneliness and protest against a world full of wickedness. Their spirituals told of the tormented souls who languished in German prisons. After the conclusion of the service, a light lunch would be shared consisting of fresh fruits and vegetables. There were fields of carpeted corn, tobacco, soybean as far as the eye could see.

Upon this beautiful landscape the American Revolution was fought. Many skirmishes between the British redcoats and the Continental Army were brought to the doorsteps of the Amish farmers. One such incident involved the unthinkable; a cherished Holy Bible was stolen from an Amish church in Berks County. The congregation was concerned that it might indeed be the work of the devil himself.

Now at that time, there resided a woman who grew herbs that could cure just about anything that might ail you. Mary Jung was her name, but everyone knew her as Mountain Mary. Not only was Mountain Mary known as an herb doctor, but she had the ability to break any spell cast by a witch. Through the Amish grapevine, it was revealed that two brothers, had taken the Holy Book, and were deemed to be possessed. The bishop contacted Mountain Mary and instructed her to visit the boy's home. Shortly after her arrival, she began to read passages from the Bible that broke the witch's spell on the brothers. Mountain Mary was considered a *powwower*, a Cherokee word which means "one who possesses the power over black magic and voodoo."

At the exact hour of the day that the brothers were being dispossessed by Mountain Mary, a fire suddenly began inside the very Amish church from which the Holy Bible was taken. All the farmers formed a bucket brigade to fight the fire, but it was in vain. The church was burned to the ground; nothing of valve inside could have been saved. Some believe that it was the work of the devil in retaliation against Mountain Mary for saving the brothers' souls.

This series of unfortunate events is what compelled the Amish to migrate west into the Great Smoky Mountains.

~ ~ ~

It was time to baptize the teenagers into the Amish faith. Minister Crowder, followed in procession by the deacons, escorts Monroe, David, and Timothy to the river where the members of the church are assembled. The boys remove their shirts and fold their arms across their chest. The deacons stand behind each of them as Crowder places his hands upon them. Ever so gently he pushes them backwards as they are lowered into the waters by the deacons.

"I baptize you with the waters of the heavenly spirit, judge not that ye be judged." As the minister spoke these words, the boys are submerged beneath the cool waters. Then they are assisted by the deacons back to the shore. "You will comply according to the *Ordnung* so help you

God."

"Amen I will," the boys reply.

"The *Ordnung* is an unwritten set of traditions which if broken shall banish thee from the Amish community," the minister advises the newest members.

"We promise to obey all the laws by which our faith is based on," the boys in unison respond. It was a time to celebrate as Conestoga wagons that are filled with bales of hay are unloaded to provide a place to sit on such a beautiful Sunday afternoon.

Ida Mae has rounds to make as she presents the red bonnets to Rebecca, Abagail, Hester, and Mabel. "Meet me inside the stable three minutes after sundown. I have something to show you," she tells them. They are curious, what could it be?

They would soon find out. One by one they enter the stable, then Ida Mae closes the door behind them. "Form a circle and let us begin."

Once they surround Ida Mae, she asks them to be seated. The horses in the stalls shake their heads, tails swatting away the flies. One mare kicks at the slats of the stall. "Now don the red bonnets and close your eyes," instructs the old woman, which they do without question.

Ida Mae opens the quilted bag and removes four dolls, one for each of them. They take them from her to hold. "Feel the power you now possess, nothing can stop it." The black woman holds a handful of needles that she distributes to them. "If and when you desire, if someone has hurt you, jab a needle into the doll, then call out the name of the one you want to punish."

Mabel removes the blackened cork stopper from her apron, smears her face with it and then does the others. "Here we are, my black witches of Dutch Bottoms," Ida Mae proclaims. The door to the stable opens. Ida Mae spreads her arms and the door slams tightly shut. "What I was gifted at my birth, I now hand down to you a coven to be reckoned with. Close your eyes and listen only to the sound of my voice -- one, two, three, you are now under my spell. I will give you a command to remember for another time. Recite with me. I do this for you, Oceeannalee."

"I do this for you, Oceeannalee," they echo her words.

"Very well, my young witches. Now when I say one, two, three, you will awake and remember nothing except the command. One, two, three," the girls open their eyes.

In their hands are the dolls that Ida Mae gave to them. "Where did you ever get these?" Hester asks her.

"I made them, just like my mammy and her mammy before. All the pretty white girls got pretty white dolls to play with, but dirt poor black tar babies don't get anything to amuse us with." She removes a doll from the quilted bags and holds it to her heart. "This is my only possession I have to remember my childhood. Those times were bad, real bad. I can still hear the crack of the whip in the hand of the master as he took out his anger on a little boy ... he couldn't have been any more than four, maybe five."

She looks at them with contempt. "What do you know of misery? You have no idea what it means to be a slave, a black slave. Yes, master; yes, ma'am; no, master; no, ma'am; all your life waiting on others at their beck and call. Well, that's all about to change, yes sir, and won't that be just fine and dandy."

The stable door is opened by Meecham Broom. The blacksmith is carrying an ax. "What are you girls doing here, you're supposed to be fixing supper by now." He looks at Ida Mae holding the doll. "And you, get your black ass out of my stable or I'll --" he threatens her with the ax.

Ida Mae takes a hatpin and sticks it into the doll's chest. Meecham drops the ax, then falls to his knees clutching his chest. He has trouble breathing. She pushes the pin again and Meecham's eyes roll up.

Mabel snatches the doll from her and pulls out the pin, just in time. A few seconds more, he would surely die. Ida Mae steps past the blacksmith, closes her bag, then leaves the stable.

The girls help Meecham to his feet. "Are you alright?" Abigail asks him.

He rests on one knee as he tries to regain his strength. "What are you doing with that black bitch? And why are you wearing red bonnets and why are your faces black as the ace of spades? And what are these little dolls for?" His mind is running on at a quick pace, trying to come to grips with a close call that almost took his life.

"The bonnets and the dolls were given to us as gifts from Ida Mae. That is all we know, Mister Broom," Hester replies.

"Well, you better get rid of them right away. You saw with your own eyes how much power she possesses. I swear she is a witch and if you are in league with her, you will be burned at the stake. Is that what you want, to die by being condemned as being a witch?"

"No of course not, sir. We will do as you wish, but please keep this just between us. If word gets out to the neighbors and our families it will be devastating to all."

"Amen, Mabel Crowder. Now scoot, all of you. What happened in the stable is for only us to know." They start to leave the stable, "Abagail, you stay behind. We need to talk, just the two of us as father and daughter."

"Yes, Father."

14

AS LONG AS THERE was daylight Cassidy was allowed to take Flea into the woods. That is, Brennon and Bonnie made sure to it that all of the boy's chores were done first before he could go. The boy was determined to locate the lost Spanish treasure that was buried more than two centuries ago.

Dutch Bottoms is flat, a great place for planting and raising livestock, but it is not a likely place for someone if they wanted to bury a treasure chest. The place that would be ideal is back in the Smokies where the coves are deep and winding, the forest thick and dense.

"You keep your eyes out for any Injuns, Flea, that might be lurking in the woods while I investigate this here trail. You can never tell who traveled before us, once upon a time."

Flea wags his tail as Cassidy ventures down the seldom-used trail. The boy takes notice that there are notches on some of the trees that could have been made by someone to guide them through the mountains. He remembers when the Cherokee kidnapped him and the women from the cornfield. Could this be the same trail that they traveled?

Flea barks, causing Cassidy to turn around. "What's got your attention?"

In the cemetery stands Ida Mae at the old hickory tree where he found the leather pouch. "What do you think she's doing there, snooping around I bet. I don't like her one bit. She's up to no good."

The old woman looks around to make sure nobody is watching. She places a knotted handkerchief into the hole of the tree, then she makes her way back home on the other side of the colony.

As soon as she is out of sight, Cassidy dashes to the tree, curious to find out what was left behind. He sticks his arm inside the tree and grabs for the handkerchief. He suddenly feels a sharp pin prick to his finger. He grimaces in pain and leaves the handkerchief in the tree. His finger has a drop of blood where the pin pricked him. He sucks on the finger to stop the bleeding. Later that night, his face is pale, the infected finger swollen and red. Bonnie feels his forehead; it is very warm to her touch. Brennon tells Cassidy to open his mouth; it is beet red. He is starting to lose consciousness, eyes closed as he lowers his head on the table.

"Hurry, we don't have a moment to waste, if his fever spikes, Bonnie ..." Brennon carries his son to the bed. Cool cloths are placed all over the boy's naked body. "It will be touch and go for the next few hours. I hope to God that Cassidy doesn't have what I suspect it could be."

"Should I fetch the minister," Bonnie asks.

"Yes, go. We need all the help to save our only child."

Bonnie scurries to alert Fallow. When she returns with the minister, Brennon is applying herbs to the boy's infected finger. Cassidy is delirious, having a nightmare. "No, you stay away from me ... Flea, go get Pa ... no, don't you touch me," the boy says as he flails away with his arms at an imaginary entity. He coughs up a mouthful of phlegm.

Fallow kneels beside the bed and opens his Bible, reading a passage about Jesus healing the leper. "*A man with leprosy came to him and begged him on his knees, 'If you are willing,' he said. 'Be clean!' Immediately the leprosy left him and he was cleansed. Mark, chapter 1, verse 40 to 45.*"

Flea whimpers at the sight of the boy.

"All we can do for him is to pray. He is in God's hands."

"How could he have been so healthy and now, Lord,

please grant him mercy at death's door," Bonnie cries leaning on Fallow's shoulder. He consoles her, rubbing his hand on her arm. She sniffles and wipes her nose.

"Do you think that Cassidy may have come into contact with something while held captive by the Cherokee?" asks Brennon.

"I doubt that," says Fallow. "If that were the case then wouldn't Fidelity and Mabel have the same symptoms?"

"Correct, Fallow, The boy must have been someplace where he came across a deadly plant or perhaps an insect. Boys will be boys, always inquisitive, that is Cassidy."

At sun up, Cassidy's finger has turned black, which Brennon has feared all along. He has to tell Bonnie the bad news. "Cassidy has contracted leprosy. There is no remedy except to amputate his decaying finger if he is to survive."

Bonnie caresses her son. "Do not touch his hand, Bonnie. Be careful that you don't get the dreaded disease," advises her husband.

Brennon has Bonnie hold the boy down. He places the handle of a wooden spoon in Cassidy's mouth and instructs him to bite down. Then Brennon uses a hatchet to sever the tip of the boy's right index finger between the nail and the knuckle. Cassidy screams in pain, then he passes out. Brennon applies wood alcohol to clean the wound and wraps it tightly with herbs in a clean cloth. The child's wails cut through the stillness of the night.

Bonnie and Brennon rack their brains trying to figure out how Cassidy came down with the deadly disease. The fever breaks, and Cassidy has dodged the deadly plague that has claimed many lives. Nevertheless, he is in a lot of pain. The finger throbs. The good doctor administers balms and fresh herbs to help in the healing.

Now that Cassidy is coherent, his parents want to know who he was with and where he has been.

"I was out in the woods when I saw the old black woman

in the cemetery. She put something into the hickory tree where I found the leather pouch."

"I see, then what did you do?" Brennon asks, eyes focused on the wound, his brow furrowed.

"Well, after she left, I was curious, so I put my hand in the tree. That is when I felt a sting, like a wasp or a bee only it was neither. Whatever it was in there was round and soft. I'm sorry. I should have let it be. If I did, I'd still have all of my fingers, for sure."

Bonnie wrings the damp cloth in her hands with a vengeance. "Damn that wicked woman! Damn her for what she has done to our loving child. *Ye shall reap what ye have sowed, sayeth the Lord.*"

"When I discovered the leather pouch in the tree, she demanded it, stating that whatever is inside the cemetery belongs to her."

"She did, did she? Well don't you worry about her son we won't let you out of our sight."

"Thanks, Pa, I think that maybe that buried treasure chest just might be cursed." Flea wags his tail sitting next to the boy.

15

NOT EVERYONE IS CUT OUT to live off the land for it takes a certain personality with plenty of grit and determination. The basic necessities -- food, shelter, and clothing that is available for most folks -- makes living outdoors so vital that without a sense of purpose, one could not survive.

Duncan Edge was about as close to the Indian way of living that who was not born a red man could achieve. Edge understood their ways only too well and, if he were a Cherokee, he also might resent the encroachment of the settlers. Ever since the last encounter, he made sure to be on guard for the unexpected.

Branch Walker was the polar opposite of Edge. He was used to the finer things of life -- a good cigar, strong liquor, a pretty woman to keep him warm at night. In the wilderness, what you see is what you get. Either you hunker down or make a hasty retreat for the creature comforts. The bounty hunter attempted to pan for gold in the crystal-clear fresh waters of Cades Cove situated to the east and all the way up north to Meigs Falls. The glitter of gold in the streams caused many a fortune seeker to go mad, staking a claim, then having to defend it from interlopers. But for Walker, the only contact he had was from the Cherokee who would come to the water's edge to fill up their earthen clay pots.

Early one morning while Walker was wading knee-deep in the stream fishing for rainbow trout, a timber wolf emerges from the nearby woods. Walker has his back to the wolf as he raises the sharply tapered wooden spear above his head. The wolf closes the distance as it moves toward the stream. Not far from where Walker is standing, a young Indian woman paddles her canoe through a patch of white water rapids. Quickly she surveys the open water ahead, then she spots Walker straight ahead.

For a fleeting moment, the timber wolf blends into the landscape, with its gray and white fur. It is a large male with long limber legs, a full bushy tail, the open mouth exposing a full set of sharp white teeth, the ears shifting side-to-side attentive to any sudden movement. The tongue darts about as the wolf advances into the shallow water. There is no way for the woman to alert Walker of the impending danger because the roar of the rapids will muffle her call. A school of fish swim between Walker's legs and he spears one of them, the fish arching its back desperately to get free. The wolf is now chest high in the stream, a few yards from Walker. He turns around with the spear resting on his shoulder, his bare chest glistening with the fresh water that drips from his catch. The wolf growls at him. Walker lowers the spear to his waist in defense to keep the wolf at bay.

Closing fast is the Indian maiden paddling the canoe with vigor. If Walker has a slim chance against the dangerous wolf, he will need more than the weapon he now wields. The wolf is ready to pounce, shifting its weight to the hind legs so as to propel itself forward to attack. The Indian steers the canoe directly into the wolf's back. Then with a knife in her hand, she dives into the water. She grabs for the tail of the wolf. The wolf turns around just as Walker spears it in the neck. The wolf tries to shake itself free of the spear as the Indian's knife is plunged into the thick fur. The crystal clear water around them is turning into a pool of red blood. The timber wolf stumbles, then collapses into the water.

Walker pulls out the spear, then jabs it into the wolf's heart slaying the beast. The swift current carries the timber wolf's lifeless body down the stream. Walker places his right hand over his heart as an expression of gratitude. The Indian maiden notices the scar on his chest. She touches it with her delicate fingers. She is quite stunning, her long black hair tied back with a leather band. Her eyes are a deep brown, the lips are a shade of pink coral. She is dressed all in deerskin with a hem of fringe. On her feet are a pair of moccasins, around her wrists are decorative beaded bands. They smile knowing only too well that moments ago a predator could have taken his life. Walker reaches out to the canoe and pulls it to the riverbank and together they wade out of the water. They walk back to his campsite where he starts a fire. She retrieves from the canoe a basket of fruit and fish. Even though Walker is perhaps the first white man she has encountered, she fears him not. She is fascinated with the color of his snow white hair and beard. He allows her to touch it. He hasn't felt a woman's soft skin in so long it doesn't seem real to him.

He attempts to make small talk with her. "My name is Branch Walker. I come from far away. I mean you no harm," as he gestures with his hands. "What is your name?"

She replies in Cherokee, "I am called Hialeah. My father is Koatohee, chief of our tribe."

Walker's mind wanders back to the skirmish when they had to defend themselves in the open meadow. There is a stirring in the woods and Hialeah grabs Walker's arm. He picks up the rifle and stands fast by the fire, cocks the hammer ready to shoot if need be.

Out into the clearing riding bareback on his horse is Adahy. He pulls on the reins, then slides off the horse's back. He speaks to Hialeah. "Do you know who this white man is? We are mortal enemies. I have come to bring you back to our camp."

Hialeah is hesitant to leave with him on his terms. Walker senses the hostility. "I should have plugged you back then when I had the chance. Get back up on that horse and ride. Hialeah is welcome to stay."

As much as she wants to be with Walker, it is best that she leave. "I go now, take care of my canoe until I return." She grabs Adahy's arm to mount his horse; he kicks his heels and they ride away.

Walker stokes the fire and begins to scale the fresh fish to eat.

16

EACH AND EVERY ONE OF US has a connection to the past; no exception including Ida Mae. But she'll have to tell all about it in her own words for better or worse; different roads, same destination.

Many a traveler to America set sail from ports located in England. One of the earliest settlers was John White, his wife, their daughter Eleanor Dare, and son-in-law Ananais. They were joined on board with many who wanted to depart England due to religious persecution. After spending several days below deck because of rough seas, the passengers are taking in the fresh salt air when John White spots a whaling ship on the horizon. It is the *Neptune Jewel*. Its captain is Emmaus Fogerty, a man of distinction and wealth. From the captain's log it is noted: *"Marking the 17th hour, 19th minute charting a course north by northeast. The watch has been set port and starboard. The crew is veteran mariners who have weathered many a storm. My only hesitation is that they will live to see their families. Could this be a harbinger of things to come? The seas are calm with a slight southerly breeze which the sails are catching that will make for a pleasant night onboard. It is a new morning. The cabin boy high up in the crow's nest has spotted the leviathan of the deep. Thar she blows! Harpooners, away all boats, aye captain. The whale takes a turn, then descends into the deep. The tail is twice the size of the small flimsy boats that follow in the wake. If the whalers get too close, they will be doomed. Attached to the harpoons are lines, tightly coiled in the boats, the ends secured to a bow hook. Up she rises, look at the size of its eyes defying us to catch her. The harpooners are within striking distance. They find their marks in the sides of the whale. Its enormous lungs inhale, then it plummets beneath the briny waves. The lines unravel tracking the path deeper and deeper. The whaleboats' sterns rise while the bows are lowered by the powerful whale. The lines suddenly slacken as the whale breaks through the surface. There is blood in the ocean as a flock of seagulls converge overhead. The whale is gasping for breath as it submerges for a final plunge. The tension on the lines is apparent for they are smoking hot. The giant fish rises up through the waves until only the tail is beneath the surface. The force of the whale sprays the boats, drenching the mariners. But even though the harpoons are deeply impaled, the whale is still full of rage, not willing to be subdued. It will take most of the morning before the whale had succumbed.*

The whale will be cut into giant slabs once hoisted aboard. Then, blubber will be boiled for the valuable rich oil to be stored in cask barrels until the ship arrivals in port. Many a whaler will seal his fate battling the giant fish. Many will be buried at sea sewed up in a burlap bag laden down with cannon balls. There will be merchants on the dock who will bid on the whale oil which will be available to purchase. The whale oil will light many lamps in homes, shops, and streets.

Several months later, the English passengers at long last conclude their voyage when they arrive at Roanoke, North Carolina, in July, 1587. Eleanor Dare shortly thereafter gives birth to a baby girl who is given the name Virginia. She is to be the first child born in America. The settlers form a colony and are accepted by the natives led by Chief Maneto of the Croatan tribe.

As supplies are quickly diminishing, John White takes it upon himself to depart from Roanoke and set sail back to England. He will purchase what is needed and then return. It is a hard decision, but if he does not do it, all shall perish.

John White returns to Roanoke after 3 years and arrives on the birthday of his granddaughter intending to find a warm welcome from his family. But to his disbelief, the settlement has been deserted, plundered, and overgrown with brush. How could this be? What could have happened to them? On the palisades close to the seacoast he finds the single word CROATOAN carved into the surface and the letters CRO carved into a nearby tree. Perhaps this is a sign that the members of the colony had decided to move to Croatoa where chief Maneto's tribe resided, south of Roanoke in the Outer Banks. But just before John White was to depart, a great hurricane came through and he was forced to set sail once again to England.

No one knows what happened to the lost souls of Roanoke Island. Some speculate that a disease, maybe cholera or smallpox, infected the colony, or perhaps they were attacked by cannibals, killed then eaten, but no bones were ever found. However, there is evidence that a slave survived and managed to escape. Ida Mae is a direct descendant of that slave who was never named. That has consumed her ever since she was a little girl, right up to this very day.

17

AFTER THE NEAR DEATH of Cassidy there began a series of unexpected events throughout the colony. Several women who were pregnant had miscarriages one after the other. Then the pigs came down with the swine flu. The fabric that held every one together was being torn apart. Could it be that these signs were meant to be that God wanted to occur? Or was it something else that was causing it?

The expectant mothers were seen in the company of the young girls to whom Ida Mae gave the red bonnets and the pushpin dolls as gifts. Also they were found feeding the hogs the day before the animals became ill. The problem was apparent to Meecham, the blacksmith, but he was hesitant to divulge what he knew.

The subtle change of character went undetected by Fallow and Fidelity as Mabel became more withdrawn. She only wanted to be in the company of Abagail, Hester, and Rebecca. They were as close as sisters, their bond tougher than leather. Whenever they were together, they spoke in a code where one word would mean something else. If they wanted to mock or demean someone, they would quote a passage from the Bible and juxtapose the meaning.

The girls were getting an education from their mentor, Ida Mae. She was molding them into living breathing lily-white dolls that would do her bidding in a whisper. As they dreamed tucked inside their beds, she would rock in her chair singing an old lullaby handed down to her when she was a little girl. Her voice was heard in their dreams, opening a door into another world, one filled with gargoyles that came alive and terrorized the living to no end. These subliminal images would draw them to a tightly woven honeycomb crafted by Ida Mae, the queen bee.

Just as a seamstress creates a colorful quilt, Ida Mae is fabricating her own and when she is done the entire colony will be hers: lock, stock, and barrel. And just like the young girls who were asleep in their beds, Cassidy's imagination was on the move. The trail into the woods that was notched out needed to be taken. He and Flea would venture there shortly and the buried treasure chest at last would be found. It made perfect sense to him: After all, if the letter was left behind by the Spaniards, who else but these conquistadors could have blazed the marked trail?

The boy tosses and turns as the face of Ida Mae invades his dreams. "Go away, leave me alone," he mutters. His dream is now a nightmare. The tree limbs grab hold of him. "Give me what you found in the hickory tree and I'll let you live," he hears her say to him. He attempts to break free, but it is no use. Her course woolen mittens scratch his face as she pokes at him, moving her hands into the shirt and britches, but she comes up empty-handed.

The strong stench of decaying flesh fills his lungs. It is then that she eyes the missing tip of Cassidy's index finger. "Let that be a reminder that I could have taken your life, little boy."

As terrified as he was, Cassidy musters up a mouthful of gumption. "My pa knows what happened to me. He's probably out looking for me right about now. You'll soon see who'll be scared, you mean old rotten hag!"

Cassidy awakens in a pool of sweat. Flea is sound asleep at the foot of the bed. He can still smell the leper. It is as if she were present in the darkened room.

How could Ida Mae be so repulsive to Cassidy and yet so alluring to the young girls? Did she possess more than one personality -- one now and another shortly after? Right before their eyes, the colony was dying. First it was the hogs, now the crops were withering away, even though there was an abundance of rain and sunshine.

A meeting was held inside the church where the elders shared their concerns. "At some point I think we have to conclude that our community will survive if we have enough food to sustain us. And it is not just that which concerns me, the unborn babies that were lost are not merely a coincidence. No these acts were premeditated, I dare say. My son, my only son almost died from leprosy, all of which can be directed with certainty at Ida Mae." The good doctor wipes his damp brow.

"I have witnessed her witchcraft with my own eyes inside the stable. She held in her hand a doll which she pushed pins into that inflicted upon me unbearable pain," relates Meecham. The blacksmith paces the floor of the church, the wooden boards creaking with his every step.

"Arthur Lynch, do you have anything to say?" Fallow asks.

"My daughter Rebecca has been acting in a rather odd way."

"How so, Arthur?" inquires Brennon.

"I have heard her speaking in a foreign tongue. Candice also has witnessed it."

"I see, so all of you believe that the evidence we have shared tonight can be presented to the congregation and that by a show of hands will bring forth a trial of witchcraft?"

"Indeed we do, Fallow. This has been going on far too long. We can no longer ignore the obvious."

"Yes, I see what you mean, Meecham. We do not need another church being burned down. It all has to end here at Dutch Bottoms."

Before they are to conclude the meeting, Brennon needs to get something off his chest. "My dear friends, you have so much to lose by putting your daughters on trial for witchcraft. I only have a son so consider the ramifications, of your actions."

The next day members of the community file in one-by-one, the men dressed all in black, the long beards covering their Sunday best attire. The women escorted by the men are also dressed accordingly, their white and black bonnets covering their hair. In their hands they carry fresh flowers to cover their strong body odors.

The church is filled many stragglers have to stand; for the rest, they have to listen from outside. The windows and the doors stay open for it is so important that, the colony hears what has to be said first hand. Minister Crowder waits patiently until everyone is settled for he does not want anything to distract him from the message that's soon to be delivered. After the hymns are sung, it was now the moment of truth. All eyes are upon him as he rolls up the sleeves of his white shirt. How can he find the words to convey what needs to be said? After all that was left far behind in rural Pennsylvania, the remnants of the burning church, what could have followed them to Dutch Bottoms? Hasn't a price already been paid by the unprovoked attack at the hands of the Indians? Dear God in heaven, haven't you put us through enough? Don't we praise you and give you thanks daily from the fruits of our labor?

Fallow holds firm to the edges of the wooden pulpit. "Brothers and sisters, we are gathered in the house of the Lord to hear testimony of our fellow brethren that evil has decided to pay us a visit. An unexpected visit and it has no intention anytime soon to depart. There can be no denial that the hogs and the crops have been infected do to the handiwork of a demon. Is it by coincidence of what we cherish so dear to us, has been taken away, like a thief in the night? I led you to this place and like the twelve tribes of Israel that followed Moses in the exodus out of Egypt, you have entrusted in me. As it says in the Good Book *he without sin cast the first stone.* We are all sinners, yet indeed there are specific sins that are incomprehensible, that cannot be forgiven. Perhaps God will pardon this particular sinner for it is by their hand that has brought evil upon us. I tried to dismiss my doubts, that what cannot be explained is not for me to understand. But I was mistaken and as I was informed last evening, there have been signs that I have ignored for too long. When we gather in the harvest, do we not remove the weeds so that they will not destroy all that was planted? So too if there be non-believers among us we must root them out. To all the naysayers, there are eyewitness accounts that will provide testimony beyond a shadow of a doubt."

Bonnie Haggard stands up; Brennon nods to her where he is seated. "What Minister Crowder has stated, take it for gospel. My son almost died and it is all because of one individual." She looks all around the church, Ida Mae is not present. "Just as I expected too afraid to show her face, and all the more reason that speaks volumes to place the blame. I accuse the unredemptive Ida Mae, the leper among us."

Meecham rises to his feet. "Look no further, my brothers and sisters. I can attest for I have seen her black magic at work. She tried to kill me. If not for Mabel Crowder, I would not be here."

"Thank you, Meecham, I did not know that. Mabel has never mentioned this to me or Fidelity."

Mabel squirms in the pew next to Fidelity. She glances over to Abagail, Hester, and Rebecca for any sign of reassurance, but their faces are devoid of expression.

Candice stands up and addresses the congregation. "I think that we need to hear from Mabel. Do you have secrets that need to be told? Say now or forever hold your tongue." Candice reclaims her seat in the pew.

Rebecca shakes her head at her mother, for if Mabel remains silent, she could be held accountable in league with

Ida Mae of the charges soon to be brought forth. There is the sound of feet shuffling then mumbling among the congregants, some pushing and shoving outside the church, jockeying for a better position in order to hear the young girl.

Mabel gathers her composure, then stands to face the gathering. "It is a fact what Mister Broom has stated, however I cannot agree that Ida Mae is solely responsible for the series of unfortunate events."

Gasps and outbursts of shame fill the church. Mabel lowers her head to avoid eye contact.

There is suddenly a disturbance of sorts outside as the waves of onlooker's part. Into the church steps Ida Mae dressed in her threadbare clothes, hair matted in tightly spun curls. Those closest to her hold their noses and turn away as she makes her way to the front of the church. "For shame, look at her," one of the women comments under her breath. Ida Mae smiles as she looks in her direction.

"Are you here to defend your actions," Fallow asks her.

"My actions, what am I accused of? It cannot be fornication, not in my condition, surely not gluttony or sloth. Perhaps I purloined something of value. Do you want to see what I have tucked away inside my tattered bag?"

Those in close proximity gag and cough from the putrid odor emitting from her body. "Do you think that it was by chance that led you here to Dutch Bottoms? Who do you think was responsible for the brothers who were possessed by a demon and saw to it that the church was burnt to the ground? This land is what the Cherokee consider sacred to them. There are spirits that inhabit the woods throughout the Great Smoky Mountains."

"Which you are, a witch," a man stands and points an accusing finger at her.

Then another man stands and gestures, "Yes we have a witch, in our midst."

One after another the congregation rises up, joining in on the taunting. She takes it all in stride until she is good and ready. "You accuse me of being a witch? Well feast your eyes on your very own." Ida Mae opens the bag and as she does, Abagail, Hester, Rebecca, and Mabel stand up. They undo their black bonnets and let them fall on the pews. Then they don the red bonnets and smear their faces with blackened corks. Many of the women recoil in terror. Ida Mae then takes out the doll; the girls follow her cue and do the same.

"I do this for you, Oceeannalee." Ida Mae commands the girls to push the pins into the tiny dolls.

The members feel tiny pinpricks throughout their extremities. Fallow holds his head as Ida Mae jabs her pins into the doll's head. It is as if a hornet's nest has descended upon the church, stinging each and all.

Into the door of the church enters Cassidy and Flea. He is holding the leather pouch that contains the Spanish letter which Ida Mae covets. Her attention is detracted from holding the girls under her spell. They drop the dolls and the pins.

"Give me what is mine."

Even though Cassidy is scared stiff, he hands over the pouch to her. Ida Mae puts away her doll and the pins into the bag. At that exact moment Timothy, Monroe, and David subdue her. Through clenched teeth, she snarls, "Damn you, damn you all!"

"Take her away and lock her up in the root cellar until we decide what to do with her," Fallow commands them. It takes all of their strength to remove her from the church kicking and screaming every step of the way.

A group of men grab the girls. One of them exclaims, "They deserve the same. Throw the witches in with the leper where they can't cause any more trouble."

Fallow pushes the angry group aside. "Unhand my

daughter. I'll keep her safe."

To which one of the men reply, "A lot of good you have done. Did you not see that she and the others are possessed? Once a witch always a witch, there is no turning back."

Fallows eyes grow wide as he raises his arms and with the back of the hand slaps the man to the floor. "How dare you, disgrace the house of the Lord! These vulnerable girls were manipulated to do the witch's bidding. I witnessed it, you as well. It was not their doing, see them now. If they were truly witches, the spell they were under could never be broken."

"The minister is absolutely correct. Did you not see how Ida Mae reacted when she was held against her will? Only a disciple of Satan would act in such a fashion, refusing to be silenced in this holy place."

"Thank you, good doctor Haggard, for defending my husband. All of us must be reasonable under these circumstances. Our daughters need to know that they are loved. Please pray for them."

The man that was smacked rises to his feet rubbing his cheek, the imprint of Fallow's hand clearly visible. "By the laws of the Amish church, the girls have to be judged accordingly. I say we take a vote to have a trial to be heard on the grounds of witchcraft. All in favor say aye, all against say nay."

By a little more than a majority of one, they vote for a trial. "The ayes have it. The congregation has spoken, minister. The girls will stand trial for witchcraft."

18

MABEL LEAVES A LETTER addressed to Fallow and Fidelity. She also leaves behind her clothes after donning the Indian attire given to her by the Cherokee. She departs the home while it is still dark.

At first light, Fidelity awakens to find Mabel's empty bed. She rouses her husband and together they read her letter:

Dearest mother and father,

I have brought shame to our home so I was left with no other alternative but to leave. I have been in contact with Mohe, the Indian brave. Together we shall somehow survive. It breaks my heart that I have to say goodbye in a letter instead of giving you my love with a kiss. I will always treasure the time we spent together.

Love always, your daughter Mabel.

Fidelity breaks down and sits on the bed as Fallow tries to console her. "I will get her no matter what it takes," he tells her.

Through heavy tears Fidelity wanders aloud, "Why, tell me why, did we ever leave our home and come to this God-forsaken place? We were so much better off back east. Tell me, because I am at a loss to understand why God has put us through so much misery and heartache."

Fallow holds Fidelity, stroking her hair while silently reflecting on their loss of Mabel. Outside the community begins to stir, the sounds of voices, horses pulling wagons, doors and shutters opening, roosters crowing, and the school bell filling the air.

There is a faint knock on the door: it is Cassidy and Flea. "Good morning, Minister Crowder, Misses Crowder," he says. The boy's eyes are looking down at his bare feet.

"Cassidy, is there something we can do for you?"

In the boy's hand is a piece of parchment that he found near the hollowed out hickory tree. He gives it to Fallow to read. It is a note from Mohe addressed to Mabel, telling her where to meet him. "I was supposed to deliver this to Mabel."

Fallow crumples up the note, looks up and down the street, then grabs the boy by the scruff of his neck, pulls him inside, and shuts the door. "You knew all about the Indian and Mabel and never told us, how could you?" Fallow demands to know.

"I was told not to."

"By who pray tell?"

"By Mabel. She didn't want anyone to know in case."

"In case of what, we need to know."

"In case she would be found out and accused of being in love with the enemy, the Injun."

"Well, she is gone, thanks to you. Why didn't you tell us when this first happened? We could have somehow found a way to make her see how foolish she is, in love with an Indian. I told her when we were held captive. I also told that Indian boy to leave her be, but he was so persistent."

Fallow dons his clothes after removing the nightshirt, then pulls on his boots. He grabs for the rifle and powder horn.

"Where are you going," Fidelity asks him.

"To bring our daughter back home; here where she belongs."

"But you have no idea where she can be. If the Indian brave and she made plans to meet in the wilderness, you'll never find them."

Cassidy notices the clothes that Mabel left still lying on her bed. "I know how we can find her. My coon dog Flea has a keen sense of smell; just one sniff of her clothes by golly and Flea will follow it all the way to wherever they might be."

"Go fetch your dog, boy." Fallow opens the door; Cassidy steps outside and lets out a loud whistle, Flea scampers to him.

Flea enters the home, then smells Mabel's clothes. Fallow takes the red bonnet and tucks it into the pocket of his long coat. He kisses Fidelity goodbye. Flea takes off into the woods with Cassidy and Fallow trailing closely behind.

~ ~ ~

Demons Anvil was where they had hoped to be reunited. It was midpoint between the Cherokee camp and Dutch Bottoms. Mabel arrived first and to her surprise, instead of Mohe, Duncan Edge was inside the cave seated by a fire. He was filling his mouth with a piece of meat, the grease running down his unkempt, scraggly beard. He wipes his face with the back of his hand. "Well look who it is, aren't you a sight for sore eyes. The last time I saw you it was at Dutch Bottoms. What brings you here?"

"Hello, Mister Edge. I am to meet someone; he should be here any minute," she replies, feeling apprehensive toward Edge.

He pulls off another chunk from the deer. "Anybody that I know?"

"I think not. He isn't from the colony."

"Huh, you don't say? Okay, who is it then?" Edge wipes the knife blade clean on his pants, then stands. He smells as if a skunk sprayed him. Mabel steps back from not only the odor but the sight of him so grotesque. Edge draws closer to her, she backs away. "You know it sure gets lonely being out in these woods without seeing anyone, especially a woman. So why don't we keep each other warm, you know, until that beau of yours shows up. I promise I'll be a perfect gentleman, what do you say?"

Mabel turns her head away and gives him a polite

shove, hoping that he will get the message to leave her alone. But Edge is persistent. He grabs her, but she resists, biting him on the wrist that draws blood. He jerks his arm back, sucking on the fresh wound.

Edge grins at her, the few teeth in his mouth dripping with blood. "You sure got spunk, pretty lady, I like that you remind me of a whore back in Chicago. She could be feisty at times. But I tamed her, yes indeed, just like I'll do with you."

Mabel tries to make a hasty retreat from the cave, but Edge is a step quicker. He grabs her, then tears off her clothes and throws her to the hard ground. He pins her arms over her head and proceeds to rape her. She cries and yells, "Please don't do this, let me go. I promise I won't tell a living soul, just let me go, Mister Edge."

He continues ravishing her like a wild animal out of control. She kicks her legs trying to get him off of her. The more she resists, the more he becomes sexually aroused. When he is finished, he releases her arms and she spits in his face. "You despicable beast of a man; when Mohe gets here he'll kill you for what you did to me." She picks up the torn deerskin dress to cover her naked and bruised body.

"You were meeting up with one of them Injuns?"

She nods her head, "Yes an Indian brave."

He becomes enraged. "You call me a beast, but you would take up with a savage and become his squaw? Well now, if that doesn't beat all," Edge surmises.

Footsteps are heard approaching the cave. Mabel's eyes light up with anticipation. "You'll soon find out what a real man is. One look at me and Mohe will skin you alive."

Edge places his hands around her throat and tightly squeezes the life out of her. Mabel's face turns purple, the eyes roll up, then her body goes limp. Edge is not done; he has to scalp her to make it appear that an Indian killed her.

The footsteps are not Mohe's, but belong to Fallow,

Cassidy, and the dog. Edge exits the cave and yells to them to get their attention.

"Hello, Mister Edge, have you by any chance seen my daughter?"

Edge places his hand on Fallow's shoulder. "I don't know how to break this to you, but was she dressed in buckskin?"

"That she was, why do you ask?"

"I was out hunting. I've been living in the cave for a spell anyway. I came back to find ..."

"To find out what, Mister Edge? You're not making any sense."

"I'm sorry to tell you this, but she's dead."

Fallow is stunned. Edge's words aren't what he wanted to hear. "What do you mean she's dead? Surely you must be mistaken."

Edge lowers his arm from Fallow's shoulder. "See for yourself," He holds Cassidy back, "Boy, you stay here with me."

Fallow enters the cave but cannot believe his eyes. His only daughter has been brutally assaulted and savagely murdered. He cradles Mabel's lifeless body as he breaks down and sobs.

Mohe steps out from a copse of trees that overlooks the Demons Anvil. Fallow carries her body out of the cave. When Edge catches the sight of Mohe, he picks up Fallow's rifle and takes aim. Flea growls at the trapper. "Shut your dog up, boy!" He pulls back on the hammer, squeezes the trigger. Flea grabs hold of his pant leg, tugging back and forth.

Mohe is in close enough proximity to see Fallow and Mabel's body, her face covered in blood. He is hesitant to advance, but then Edge pulls the trigger, the bullet just barely passing over his head. Mohe drops to the grass anticipating another volley.

"That's him," shouts Edge, pointing to where he fired the rifle. "That's the one who killed your daughter. C'mon, let's go get him!" Edge pulls out his knife and takes off in hot pursuit of Mohe, who has now retreated back into the woods.

Edge's brief chase ends and he returns fully satisfied that Fallow has been duped into believing that the Indian killed Mabel. Fallow will carry her body back to the colony where it will receive the proper Amish burial.

~ ~ ~

The witch trail will have to be delayed while the community comes together to mourn one of their own. Mabel's body is washed, then wrapped in a clean white sheet and placed in a plain wooden coffin. Duncan Edge remains at Dutch Bottoms until Mabel is lowered into the ground. His last words to Fallow before he rides off are, "Whatever it takes, I'll get that Injun, so help me God."

Mohe returns to the Cherokee camp where he confides to Wise Sparrow about witnessing the girl that he loves in her father's arms. "Who could have done that to her? She was so beautiful and so filled with life. We were going to live together and raise a family. Now all of that has been taken away from me. I must find the one who took her life so I can take theirs."

Wise Sparrow listens to him, then as a grandmother would advise a grandchild she sits him down beside her. "I have lived a long time, seen the good and bad in men. Why some follow the Lord and others the devil I'll never know. But you do what you think is what Wild Honey would have wanted. I hope it will in the end bring peace to you."

As Mohe departs her lodge, he encounters Hialeah and relates to her the tragic news. "Do you think that one of the tribal members could have killed her?"

"No, I do not, for no one knew that we were to meet at the falling waters but us."

"I only saw two white men and the boy."

"Then one of them must have killed her; who else could it be?"

"One of them fired his rifle, trying to kill me. Then he came after me. I should have stayed to fight, instead of running off like a scared squaw."

"You are brave, you will live to fight another day. And you will take out your vengeance against them."

"Why did the white man ever come to our land? Why did they not stay where the Great Spirit put them? All of the trees have roots firmly planted in the earth that is just the way it is. They provide shade from the sun, the birds build their nests for their young, and many of the trees bear fruit for us to eat."

Hialeah takes his hand as they walk to the riverbank where young braves are in the process of shaping birch trees into canoes. Together they launch Hialeah's canoe into the river, then paddle down the stream.

"Where are we going?" Mohe asks her.

"I want you to meet a man who although he is not Cherokee in many ways he is."

They navigate through the white water rapids and observe beaver that are busy crafting a dam. Where the river bends, Branch Walker's cabin comes into view. A campside fire is ablaze; they see a string holding fresh-caught fish tied between two trees drying in the noonday sun.

Walker steps out from the cabin. He is shirtless, the rifle propped up by the door. Mohe and Hialeah paddle the canoe to the bank, then disembark. Walker and Mohe recognize one another, how could they not? Ever since their skirmish in the woods, protecting Fidelity, Mabel and Cassidy, enemies still. Hialeah senses their hatred, negotiates as an intermediary. Walker spits out a wad of tobacco juice at the feet of Mohe, who reacts by grabbing the handle of his tomahawk tucked in the belt around his waist.

Hialeah pats Mohe's wrist. "We did not come to fight each other."

Walker grabs the rifle and cradles it over his forearm. He spits again, this time aiming for the fire. She tells Mohe to relate what happened to Mabel forthwith.

Walker lowers the rifle, shaking his head in disbelief. "How could that happen? You say she was scalped? Who scalps women? Only a yellowbelly coward would stoop so low."

Hialeah appeals to Walker. "Will you help us find her killer?"

"I reckon, Hialeah. Heck, the Cherokee have more or less let me be ever since I've been here. If I know Fallow Crowder, he will go through the gates of hell to get at the one who killed his daughter. You said a white man shot at you?"

"Yes, and then he ran after me into the woods."

"Damn, there's only one other white man I can think of who fits that description. It has to be Duncan Edge."

19

THE PROCEEDINGS COMMENCE inside the Amish church to decide whether to condemn or dismiss charges of witchcraft against Abagail Broom, Hester Adams, and Rebecca Lynch. A moment of silence is observed for the recently departed Mabel Crowder. It is a huge undertaking, not only for Fallow but also Fidelity who are still grieving for their only child.

Deacon Tobias Sweezey, a confirmed bachelor, has been designated to preside over the proceedings so that there will be no impartiality for or against the accused. Philip Smart, the tailor, and Brennon Haggard, the doctor, are the appointed judges.

Deacon Sweezey pounds the wooden gavel on the lectern to open the proceedings. "Here ye, the Amish colony of Dutch Bottoms have voted by a majority ruling that there are grounds to try the accused as witches. How say you?"

One by one, the girls reply, "Not guilty."

While the trail begins, David, Monroe, and Timothy are dispatched to bring Ida Mae to the church. When the door to the root cellar is opened, they find to their astonishment Ida Mae is not there. She has escaped. They quickly return to the church and David announces the news.

A collective gasp fills the church. Sweezey pounds the gavel to restore order. "Who was assigned to watch her," the deacon demands an answer.

"All of us were assigned to the prisoner," Monroe replies.

"Then how is it that she is not among us? Did she have help slipping pass the watch?"

"Begging your pardon, sir, but the padlock was secured

and there was not any evidence that it was tampered with. It is as if he just vanished by magic," Timothy comments.

"Black magic, more likely. Nevertheless we have a trial to conduct," surmises the deacon.

Individually, Abagail, Hester, and Rebecca are called to take the stand and state their case. All the girls make a solid defense which squarely places their actions as sorcery directed by Ida Mae. Each and every time Ida Mae was present, their personalities dramatically changed. They became possessed against their will. And while Ida Mae was under lock and key, the girls were themselves; nothing out of the ordinary was apparent. However, it was all-apparent that if not for the manipulation of Ida Mae the leper, the girls would not be on trial for witchcraft.

"How say you?" Deacon Sweezey asks.

"Not guilty," Philip Smart replies.

"Not guilty," echoes Brennon Haggard.

"The vote is unanimous, you are free to go," concludes Deacon Sweezey.

Even though the girl's trial was decided in their favor, there still lingered a specter of fear throughout the colony. The fact that Ida Mae could have managed to escape from the root cellar convinced many that it was orchestrated by the devil himself.

Not only were the Amish superstitious, but the Indians shared a common bond. Some of the Cherokee have witnessed apparitions in the mountains of a woman near Demons Anvil. They believe it is the spirit of Oceeannalee.

The untimely death of Mabel Crowder has brought a pall to the colony. Her body wasn't yet cold in her grave when a figure that resembled her was spotted walking among the tombstones. Unexpectedly, a panic spread where even the slightest cough, fever blister or rash was construed to assume that the supernatural was afoot.

Duncan Edge has returned to his haunts, hunting for

game, mostly black bear. Now that the winter has arrived, the bears will mate, then seek out a suitable den to hibernate. Come spring, the females will have a pair of cubs to nurse and rear therefore it is expedient for Edge to place his traps before the heavy snows arrive.

Fallow and Cassidy have lost the trail that Flea was tracking. It has gone cold. Cassidy tells Fallow about the leather pouch with the Spanish letter enclosed. "If we double back, I could show you the trail where I noticed the trees notched out from an ax. I just bet that somewhere on that trail is where the Spaniard buried the golden treasure."

Fallow pats the boy's head. "Lead the way. Maybe we'll get lucky, and who knows, perhaps whoever took my daughter's life traveled this same path."

Together they traverse the trail deep into the woods paying keen attention to the trees that are notched belt high. The trail twists and turns, crossing over brooks and fallen timbers, then ascends into the mountains. Here there is a dramatic change in the weather as the temperature drops. The sun begins to set as they seek shelter for the night.

Fallow stacks kindling for a fire while Cassidy scours for something to eat. The fire is warm and toasty as a slight flurry of snow begins to fall. Through the bramble Cassidy and Flea emerge with a pair of freshly killed jackrabbits slung over the boy's shoulders.

"I must say you're pretty good with that slingshot."

Cassidy drops the rabbits by the fire while Flea curls up shaking off the wet snow. Fallow and Cassidy remove the fur from the rabbits and share the dinner with the dog.

Fallow can't help but notice the condition of the boy's feet. He removes any semblance of the rabbits flesh from the fur, then directs Cassidy to slip his feet into the warm fur. It is the first time he has ever not been bare foot, a wonder of wonders much appreciated.

113

The snow intensifies, muffling the stirrings of the creatures in the woods. Fallow and Cassidy hunker down for the night, staying vigilant so the fire will not die. Come first light, they will break camp and proceed to the base of Thunderhead Mountain. Fallow informs Cassidy that this is the end of the trail for them. From here on out, the climb will become much more difficult with each step of the way and if the heavy clouds in the sky are any indication, they could be trapped in a blizzard.

Flea becomes distracted by a stirring in the bushes. He barks, then dashes off. Cassidy calls out to Flea, but the dog is now out of sight. "I'll go get him and be right back."

Fallow watches him while he cocks the trigger of the rifle in case they are being set up in a trap by the Indians.

"Minister Crowder, come here real quick. I think I found something."

Fallow follows Cassidy's voice to where the boy is waiting. "What did you find?" he asks.

Flea is busy pawing the ground, removing pebbles and twigs that cover an object buried in the woods. Cassidy drops to his knees and uses his hands to reveal what is hidden from sight. "Do you think it might be the Spanish treasure?"

"I don't know, but we'll soon find out."

What Flea has found for his master is not the buried treasure, but a wooden coffin containing the remains of a Spanish conquistador. The skeleton is clothed in a uniform possibly that of an officer. A metal helmet covers the skull. The leather boots show signs of decay, and around the waist is a belt with a cutlass in a scabbard. Tucked inside the tunic, between the brass buttons, is a leather pouch. Carefully Cassidy removes it from the skeleton. Remarkably, it resembles the one he found in the hickory tree at the cemetery.

"Go ahead, Cassidy, open it and let's see what it has

inside to tell us."

It is a letter written in Spanish that bears the same seal affixed in red wax at the bottom of the parchment. The handwriting however, is not the same. "Can you make out what it says," Cassidy asks Fallow.

"I cannot for I do not speak or read the Spanish language. But the fact that it was buried with this soldier tells me that it must be important and not meant for anyone to read."

"So it was meant to be kept a secret?"

"Maybe this soldier knew the whereabouts of the buried golden treasure and so to keep him quiet they killed him."

"Cassidy, I must say you possess quite an imagination. When we were inside the cave hiding out from the Indians all those skulls and bones piled up, I now think that maybe the gold has something to do with it."

Cassidy snaps his fingers. "Exactly what I'm thinking." Then as quick as a smile crosses his face, it now turns into a frown. "We have no map to help us find it."

"Don't get down in the mouth, son. Maybe we will, then again maybe we won't. That is what life is all about."

They close the coffin and Fallow says a prayer, then they set off back to Dutch Bottoms.

~ ~ ~

Bonnie paces back and forth inside the residence, periodically glancing out the window. Brennon buttons his coat, then sits at the table. "Where can he be? He should have been home by now," she says. "Why did you allow him to take off with Fallow in the first place? You know how unstable the minister can be. Sakes alive, they just laid to rest their only child, he should be home with Fidelity for goodness sake."

The door opens and in scampers Flea followed close behind by their son. He hardly has time to say hello when Bonnie grabs him by the earlobe. "Where have you been, child? My God, you smell worse than that coon dog. Off with your clothes and what is that covering your feet?"

"That is rabbit fur. They kept my toes warm when it snowed up in the mountains."

"The mountains, what were you doing up there?"

Cassidy strips off his clothes, stands naked as a jaybird as Bonnie takes the oaken bucket to draw water from the well. "Pa, you should have been with us."

"Did you find out who killed Mabel?"

"Sad to say, nope. But we did find a soldier, a Spanish officer who was buried, and he had a leather pouch with a letter just like the one I found in the old hickory tree."

"Really, Cassidy, where is it?"

Cassidy rifles through his pile of dirty clothes just as his mother returns with the bucket of water. Bonnie dips a clean cloth into the bucket and proceeds to wash her son. Brennon opens the leather pouch dons his reading glasses to peruse the letter.

"What does it say, Pa? Anything about where we can find the buried treasure?"

"Buried treasure, are you still consumed with finding what doesn't belong to you?"

"Now Bonnie, let the boy be. This letter is rather peculiar. It is very troubling to say the least."

"How so, Pa," Cassidy asks his father while Bonnie scrubs him with a stiff coarse hairbrush to remove the layers of crud and dirt.

"I can only imagine what the good Minister Crowder must look like, if you are any indication to my eyes." She gives Cassidy a dry pair of clothes to wear.

The boy sits next to his father at the table. Brennon concludes reading the letter, then removes the glasses. "So what did the letter say, Pa?"

"It was a warning addressed to Juan Pardo from Hernando Moyano, a sergeant of the Spanish army. He warns of an impending doom that no matter how many garrisons Juan Pardo has at his disposal, this particular enemy will not be defeated."

"Do you think, Pa, that the body was of that Sergeant Moyano?"

"I would say the probability is highly unlikely. I tend to think that this particular letter was written prior to the one that you found in the cemetery. Sergeant Moyano is the only one who survived whatever it was that killed the other soldiers."

"There were piles of skulls and bones in the cave where we hid from the Injuns. Maybe they were the remains of the soldiers."

"They very well could be. It is plausible."

Bonnie dries her hands on the apron. "Hogwash, to all of that tripe, and by the way, who cares about the dead, anyway? Brennon Haggard you are a doctor, your lot in life is to make folks well. You are not in the business of putting the deceased into the ground. Let the dead rest in peace, that is where they belong. Don't go digging through the graveyard when you certainly have no business being there."

Cassidy's index finger that had the tip removed still gives him pain at times -- and now it is acting up. He puts his hands in the pocket of the britches.

"It still brings you discomfort?" Brennon asks.

"That it does, Pa."

Bonnie shakes her head. "That hideous troll of a woman, may she rot in hell for all the misery she has brought, not only to our home, but to the colony."

"She has a way of getting under one's skin."

"Amen, Pa. I hope I never see her again."

Bonnie smiles while cleaning Cassidy's dirty clothes, happy to know that Ida Mae is no longer at Dutch Bottoms.

~ ~ ~

Minister Crowder enters his home, Fidelity sits in the far corner of the room where the shadows of the day conceal her. Fallow removes his hat, brushes off the dust from the trail. "What are you doing sitting there in the dark?" he asks.

Her attention is focused outside the window. "Ever since Mabel was buried, there has been a crow perched on the church steeple. It stares at me with those cold black piercing eyes. I know that if I step outside, it will swoop down and pluck my eyes out."

Fallow kneels down in front of her and takes her hand to hold. "Fidelity, you must let it go. Mabel is gone and she is now in Heaven. Have no fear of a bird that has no threat to harm you."

"God in his infinite wisdom created us for what purpose? Just to take us whenever he sees fit? We are better off building castles of sand than to pay homage to a God who is nothing more than a sadist. Would I do that to him? Would I have taken the flesh and blood of His child? Answer me that, Fallow Crowder?"

"I have no answer to give to you. Don't you think I haven't struggled trying to comprehend the Grand Design of why God does what he does? Why would he allow Mabel to die when she had a full life ahead of her? Why allow a killer to live, to walk among us and take her life? I cannot come to terms with all of it."

Fidelity walks back to the window and peers out. "I want to leave Dutch Bottoms and return back east for that is where we belong. This dreadful place has no attraction for me. It has taken Mabel, my heart, my soul."

"If that is what you wish, then so be it," her husband replies. "I will notify Deacon Sweezey first thing in the morning. Now you must confront the present and let go of the past."

20

WALKER, MOHE, AND HIALEAH arrive at Dutch Bottoms where Timothy greets them at the gate, recently installed ever since the Cherokee raid. "We come in peace. May we enter?" Walker asks.

Timothy is apprehensive because the last time he encountered Mohe, they were in the middle of a bloody battle. "You can enter only if you surrender your weapons. Otherwise state your business where you stand."

Walker translates Timothy's words to the Indians. They refuse to give up their weapons. Walker understands their concern and so they shall wait while he passes through the gate. Once inside, he relinquishes the long rifle, the powder horn, and the pistols, plus the hunting knife, to Timothy. "I need to see Minister Crowder. Is he here?"

"Yes, he has just arrived. He was out on the trail trying to find the killer of his daughter Mabel."

"I see." He points to Mohe: "This Indian who was our enemy was in love with her. He and the Indian squaw Hialeah have offered their help in finding her killer."

"How do you know, Mister Walker, that he in fact didn't kill her? I don't trust him."

Walker places his hand on Timothy's shoulder. "Son, I've been through many a fight in my lifetime. I have a pretty good way of figuring out an adversary's intent before they do. Other than that arrow that put a hole in my chest, I'd say I'm doing okay."

"Well, be that as it may, but I'll be keeping my eyes on them until you leave."

Walker enters the Crowder home where Fallow and Fidelity are pleased to see him. He and Fallow waste no time bringing one another up to speed as Fidelity prepares a meal. Together they break bread and share a bottle of wine.

"If it is alright with you I want to pay my respects to your daughter. We went through a lot, Mrs. Crowder, in able to see you safely home. And if God is my judge, I'll see to it that I bring peace to you and your husband with the capture or death, whichever may be, to who did this to her."

Walker bids them farewell and informs Fallow that he will be camping for the night outside the walls of the colony. Come sun up, with or without Fallow, Walker and the Indians will set out to track down Mabel's killer.

For Fidelity to travel back east was wishful thinking. Fallow's return would be an act of desperation. He would be seen as a loser, once a leader to be admired, now just another vagabond lost in wanderlust. But try as he must to convince Fidelity to stay was an ordeal.

Fallow seeks out council with Doctor Haggard to see if there is something he could prescribe to break her depression. How many poor souls were left to fend for themselves without a doctor to help overcome their pain because they were never psychoanalyzed? So with the good doctor's help, Fidelity came around. She became good as new back to her own self. The search for Mabel's killer would have to wait until another time. It will be up to Walker and the Indians to track him down.

As much as Fallow wanted to go with them, he knew that his place was with his wife.

~ ~ ~

Duncan Edge keeps the memory of that day fresh in his mind and so he won't let his guard down. Most killers are driven to repeat the act over and over until they bite the dust.

Hialeah's father, Chief Koatohee, has dispatched a dozen braves to find her. She has not been seen since leaving the campgrounds with Mohe. The scouting party paddle their canoes down the Oconaluftee River which passes through the valley heading south, where they find Walker's cabin. To their surprise, she is not there. The braves decide to split up; Tsiyi will lead one group to Cosby Nob, the hunting grounds of the Cherokee, while Adahy will lead the others to Clingmans Dome, the highest point in the Smoky Mountains.

It is truly an insurmountable undertaking in so much that Mohe is one of the best trackers in the tribe and Hialeah has inherited her father's genes to be self-sufficient to survive.

~ ~ ~

Rebecca, Hester, and Abagail are inside the barn where the eyes of the colony cannot see them. Although it has been several weeks since the trial for witchcraft had found them not guilty, they have been looked upon with suspicion. Several of the women have their doubts about them and let their feelings known by not mincing words.

"We haven't much time before the men return with the livestock," whispers Abagail as she keeps her eyes focused on the barn door.

Hester fakes a swoon covering her forehead with the back of her delicate hand. "I do have a hankering for Timothy Smart. He is so handsome with those big blue eyes I could just drown in, not to mention he is strong as an ox."

"Well, I do declare, there is a hot breeze blowing that's turning your face red as a cherry," exclaims Rebecca. The girls all share the joke. "So who do you fancy Abagail?"

"Oh, I don't know. All the boys act the same, I have no preference one way or the other."

"Well, I have my eyes set on your brother David. I know he is quiet and shy, but he'll come around, that I will make sure of."

"Hester Adams, you leave my brother alone. You take those thoughts from your head this very minute!" Abagail demands stomping her foot in a sign of protest.

"Now wouldn't that be something if our brothers married us, then we would all be one big family," suggests Rebecca.

"Be gone with all of that talk, we are here for more important matters." Hester points to the hayloft and one-by-one they climb the wooden rungs up to the loft. Hidden behind the neatly stacked bales of hay is what they have come for. Inside a knotted tablecloth are the red bonnets and the pushpin dolls. Hester unties the knot, then they don the bonnets and hold the dolls close to their breasts.

"Mabel should be here with us."

"She is present in spirit, I can feel her presence."

"We will never forget her, no matter how old we are, no matter where we may be."

The girls form a circle, holding hands and closing their eyes. They take deep breaths, then chant the words told to them by Ida Mae. "*I do this for you, Oceeannalee.*"

They commence a séance to connect with the spirit of Mabel, but instead it is Ida Mae who comes through to them. Deep in the woods, Ida Mae's ears are ringing. She smiles nodding her head. "Yes, I hear you loud and clear, my fair maidens, witches of sorcery. Now listen, pay close attention to the message from my lips to your ears."

The moment is interrupted by the sounds of the clanking of cowbells as the livestock are being herded into the barn by their brothers. "Hurry, we have to hide the dolls and bonnets before they see us," Abagail comments as she collects the items. She then places them into the tablecloth ties the knot and covers it with the bales of hay. They have barely enough time to climb down from the loft before the animals arrive.

The sisters and brothers cross paths without a word spoken. Once they are outside the barn, Hester plucks a few strands of straw from Rebecca's hair. They share a laugh.

The voice of Ida Mae still echoes in their ears. "Who would have thought that we could conjure up the spirit of Mabel to communicate with us, but a portal opened which allowed Ida Mae to enter?"

"Do you think she is deceased?"

"Perhaps. Isn't that the purpose of a séance, to be able to conjure up the undead?"

"Why do you think that we have this power that no one else possesses?"

"Good questions, Abagail and Rebecca. Unfortunately I do not know why, but we must be discrete in our activities. I have heard that women accused of practicing sorcery have been killed by being hanged or tied to a stake and burnt to death or crushed by piling stones one-by-one on the body until every bone has been broken."

"Puritans, who do they think they are? They preside over a kangaroo court, then decree by a higher power to be duly obligated to cleanse the demons from the innocents."

The girls dispense, knowing it is better not to be seen together. Otherwise a specter of doubt could be construed from the elders, especially Deacon Sweezey. He has foisted animosity towards them ever since the decision of the trial was rendered in their favor. He is out to get them. He detests the fact that the girls consider him hideous and homely. Deep down inside, he covets sinful desires for each of the girls. If he cannot have them, then no other man will either. He will see to it if only in his dreams.

21

WALKER, MOHE, AND HIALEAH spot white clouds of smoke in the clear sky above the treeline not far from Deep Creek. Mohe advises them to be on the lookout for any sudden movement because they could be walking into a trap.

Attached to several trees is a trip-line positioned at the height of a boot and cleverly camouflaged with leaves twigs and bush. Any sudden motion of the trip-line will alert Duncan Edge that trespassers are within striking distance.

Carefully they tread with each step advancing closer to the cabin. Mohe spots the trip-line, but it is a split second too late to warn Hialeah. She activates the bear traps that spring shut, startling her. The door to the cabin opens, followed shortly thereafter by gunfire.

Walker leaps to where she is. They dive for cover within a split hair of the bullet taking one of their lives.

Mohe throws his tomahawk at Edge, but it lodges deep into the log above the door. Edge drops the rifle and pulls out the hunting knife. Mohe rushes at him, remembering the last time he encountered this white man who was attempting to kill him. The Indian wasn't about to allow Edge the opportunity to fire off another shot. Unarmed, he has to somehow get the knife away from Edge.

Walker calls to him, "Mohe, he is my friend, he will not harm you!" Walker's words fall on deaf ears. Mohe and Edge wrestle for control of the knife. Walker rushes to them, having no choice but to use the stock of the rifle to knock Edge off Mohe.

The trapper shakes off the blow from the rifle and places Mohe into a chokehold, then begins to squeeze.

Hialeah picks up a heavy stone and smashes it over Edge, the impact splitting his head open. He collapses in a pool of blood, while Mohe coughs trying to catch his breath.

"Is he dead?" Hialeah asks with a hint of concern.

Walker kneels down, holding the trapper's chin, shaking it back and forth. "Nope, he's not dead. But you snuffed out his flame, that's for sure."

Mohe pulls the tomahawk from the splintered log and tucks it back into his belt. He points to Edge. "He is the one that I saw the day Wild Honey was killed. He tried to kill me."

Walker taps him on the shoulder. "Keep an eye on him while I take a look inside the cabin."

The cabin is sparsely furnished a chair, table, and makeshift cot. In the corner is a pile of furs and beaver pelts. Walker tosses them aside to find assorted scalps. Walker is puzzled. Why would Edge be collecting them, for what purpose? What else could Edge be hiding that he doesn't want anyone to find out about regarding his past?

As he is leaving the cabin, a shiny object catches his eye next to the foot of the cot. It is a silver chain that holds a locket bearing the engraved letters *MC*. Walker pulls out the folded up poster of the killer back in Chicago. He now has his doubts once again in regards to Edge.

Walker retraces his steps to where Edge has now regained consciousness. Mohe holds the trapper's rifle aimed at Edge's chest. Walker drops the scalps in front of Edge and opens his hand that holds the silver chain and locket. He waits for an explanation, but the trapper merely grins up at him, then darts a glance at the Indians. "They'll fetch top dollar back east, for sure worth more than a buffalo hide."

Mohe cocks the hammer, then pokes the end of the barrel into Edge's chest. "Indians don't scalp people randomly to trade as a trophy. We only scalp our enemies."

Edge looks deep into Mohe's eyes. "Is that right? Then why did you kill the women and men back at Dutch Bottoms, then mutilate and scalp them? Enemies my foot, you gave them no chance whatsoever to defend themselves. You attacked, snuck up on them in the dead of the night."

Walker drops the wanted poster next to the scalps. "I still think you are the killer of Brad Clifton and I suspect you are also responsible for Mabel Crowder's untimely death, butchered like an animal."

Edge takes in a couple of deep breaths, the blood from his wound running down the back of the head. He dabs his dirty hands, applying pressure to stem the flow. "It was in self-defense. I just left the card game and was confronted by that sore loser, Clifton. Like a coward he lurked in the dark shadows and got the jump on me. He pulled a gun and demanded the money I won fair and square. We tussled a bit, then the gun went off. I knelt down next to him, but he was a goner. Next thing I know, an officer of the law is blowing his whistle and running toward me."

"So you ran. Why didn't you stay and explain what happened?"

"It all happened so fast, I wasn't thinking except to run for my life." Edge looks at Mohe who still has the rifle pointed at him.

"He was there, Snow Hair. I saw him with the girl from the village. "

"Damn heathen Injun, they're nothing but trouble. You can't trust them, no matter how hard you try. So what's the story with her? She's pretty for a squaw you might say."

Hialeah steps closer to Walker, who puts his arm around her waist, pulling her in closer. "Hialeah is mine I've never been treated better by another woman before." He gestures toward Mohe. "You accuse him of killing

Mabel. Why would he take her life? He loved her?"

"Love, what a crock of beans. What do they know about it?"

"They treat one another with respect, something that you know nothing about."

Emerging from the woods is Adahy and the Cherokee braves who quickly surround the campsite prepared to fight if necessary.

"Adahy, what are you doing here?"

"Your father, Chief Koatohee, was worried when you did not return. He sent us to find you and bring you back."

"Tell him I am not in danger. I have no need of a chaperone. Tell him I will return on my terms, not his."

Adahy steps closer, then places his hand around her wrist. She resists, then Walker intervenes. "Take your hand off her. Hialeah isn't going anywhere."

The situation quickly escalates. Mohe tries to defuse the tension between them. "I will safeguard her passage back to the camp. Go now and tell Koatohee that his daughter has been found."

The braves close in. Only Mohe is armed, so the odds are highly stacked against them.

Adahy notices the wound to Edge. "What happened to him?"

"I hit him with a rock," Hialeah replies. To which all of the braves laugh with delight.

"So what will you do with the white man?" To which Walker replies, "He will be brought to trial back east but before that happens, I will deliver him to the murdered daughter's father."

Adahy and the Cherokee braves were not about to leave without the chief's daughter, so a compromise is hastily arranged. The trapper's furs will be used as a gesture of good faith that would appease Chief Koatohee until Hialeah returns. What could have quickly escalated into a bloodbath was averted in a way that allowed all to walk away as winners.

Walker ties Edge's hands behind his back, then they set out for Dutch Bottoms where Fallow will decide his fate.

22

CASSIDY IS BUSY BURNING the midnight oil, seated at the table. In front of him are the letters and a piece of paper with a quill. Dutifully he dips the tip of the quill into the ink holder.

Brennon stirs in his bed and then tosses off the covers. He makes his way into the kitchen. Through bleary eyes he can barely make out his son. "What is keeping you up so late at this hour of the night?"

"I'm trying to figure out where the buried treasure is." Cassidy has created a map that depicts Dutch Bottoms in the west, Thunderhead Mountain in the east and Demons Anvil to the north.

"That's a lot of territory to cover, son, don't you think?"

"That it is, Pa. I'd guess it is ten miles to Thunderhead Mountain, another ten to Demons Anvil give or take, so to carry a chest loaded with gold the conquistadors could not know have traveled much further than here." Cassidy places a large X on the map.

"You'll make a fine surveyor when you get older, son."

"Pa, why do you think Ida Mae is so interested in all of this?"

"That is a tough question, one I do not know the answer to. One day she just arrived unannounced back east. She would not divulge her previous whereabouts to a living soul. And when we pulled up stakes she did as well. Ida Mae is like a bad penny that you cannot get rid of and nobody will take it from you in trade."

All of their talking has stirred Bonnie. "Both of you get back into bed and turn off the lamp. It will be sun up before shortly."

~ ~ ~

Adahy returns to the camp, then enters Chief Koatohee's lodge. He presents the furs and pelts, but the chief is incensed and demands to know, "Where is my daughter? I told you to bring her back to me. Instead you shower me with this?"

Adahy is at a loss for words.

"If she will not come to me, then I will go to her and drag her back to where she belongs. Where is she, Adahy?"

"Hialeah is with Mohe and Snow Hair. They had another white man who these furs belonged to."

Koatohee summons Chief Oconostota to a powwow where they will decide what path to follow. A council vote will be cast by the entire camp. The chiefs have expressed by decree to ensure Hialeah's swift return to the fold. If anyone stands in their way, there will be no survivors. Inside the council lodge, one after the other cast a vote for war.

When Wise Sparrow takes a stand to vote against war, she is admonished and shouted down, her concerns falling upon deaf ears. She will not be silenced as she shouts to the council members, "Mohe has not returned and Adahy has testified that Hialeah is with him. Please allow them time and eventually they will come home."

"Enough time has already passed. If we do not react, the white man will bring more of their kind to our land. The Great Spirit gave this land to us, not to the white man. We have been the guardians, the caretakers for many moons, respectful of Brother Sun, Sister Moon, Mother Earth. The intruders come to take, not to give or to share. Now my daughter Hialeah has fallen into their trap, their way of thinking in place of the Cherokee."

The meeting concludes as war whoops fill the lodge by the braves who disperse eager to take on the warpath. They sharpen the tomahawks, the arrows, and the lances, then smear warpaint onto their faces and the horses. Disheartened by what she cannot vision, Wise Sparrow is filled with pain and sorrow in her heart, knowing that hatred for one another only begets more of the same. Will the perpetual circle of war, death, and sorrow ever be broken?

23

IT IS ALMOST SUNRISE. The darkness of the night slowly fades away from the tall timbers as Walker, Mohe, Hialeah, and Edge arrive at Dutch Bottoms.

David Broom is standing guard at the gate. He cocks the hammer of his rifle. "Halt and be recognized before I raise my gun and fire it at you."

"Save your powder, son. We mean you no harm," replies Walker with his hands in the air. "See for yourself, we need to speak with Minister Crowder."

David lowers the rifle, relieved that it is not a ruse for him to unlock the gate. He opens it to let them enter, although he is wary of the Indians who are carrying weapons.

"Don't fret son, they are on our side. I'll vouch for them," says Walker as he nudges Edge forward.

David secures the gate and takes up his post. They arrive at Crowder's doorstep and Walker knocks on the front door. The darkness inside the home is soon illuminated by the lighting of a lamp. Fallow is still in his nightshirt when he opens the door. He is surprised to see them, especially Edge.

"Morning, Fallow. Sorry to wake you so early before the sun is up, but I promised you I would deliver who was responsible for your daughter's death."

He grabs Edge by the arm so that he can be face-to-face with the minister.

Fallow looks confused. "Surely you are mistaken, Walker. The trapper found her in the cave."

"He killed and scalped her, then placed the blame on the Cherokee. I found a collection of scalps in his cabin that he was going to sell as souvenirs to the folks back east."

Fallow glares at Edge with disdain. "Is what Walker describes to me the truth?"

"I don't deny that I scalped some of my enemies, but as God is my judge I did not touch a hair on your beautiful daughter's head. Only an animal could have done that." Edge turns his head toward Hialeah and Mohe, hoping to draw Fallow's attention away from him and cast a shadow of a doubt on him being accused in Mabel's death.

By using sign language, Mohe communicates with Walker who interprets his words to Fallow: "I loved Wild Honey with all of my heart. We knew that the white man and the Cherokee would not approve of the union between us. So we planned to meet and run away."

Walker turns to Hialeah, who is beaming with pride; her love for him is all so evident. "I can sympathize for I too love an Indian woman. I would lay down my life for her, that is how strong my feelings are for her."

Fallow paces in front of them as he tries to come to grips with what has thus far transpired.

"So what do you suggest we do with Edge? Try him here or else I'll transport him back to Chicago and claim the bounty that has been placed on his capture. It makes no difference to me, just as long as he gets what's coming to him."

Fidelity is still half-awake when she comes to the open door and sees them. "Is that you, Mabel? You have finally returned?" She possesses a look of bewilderment. "Why are you wearing those clothes? Come inside and change into the more suitable attire before our neighbors take notice."

Fallow holds his wife closely. "Fidelity, this is not Mabel -- she is dead. Don't you remember when we buried her not so long ago?" Fallow looks at the others. "She hasn't been the same ever since then. She is now taking medication."

Fidelity holds a pair of knitted baby booties close to her

heart, a reminder of when Mabel was an infant. The medication has definitely taken a toll as the mood swings have her drifting in and out of reality. "Who is the Indian brave, Mabel? Have I met him before?"

"This is Mohe, Chief Oconostota's nephew -- a Cherokee brave," Walker tells her.

Felicity tries to comprehend what he is telling her, but to no avail. "I recall an old woman who was blind and held captive. You remember her, Mabel, don't you? Oh what was her name?" She stares at Hialeah. "My mind is not as sharp as it once was."

Edge fights with the restraints around his wrists, his face filled with pent-up rage. Walker pokes him in the ribs with the barrel of his gun. "We'll get to you, sure as hell has Lucifer as the keeper of the gates."

Walker has waited for the opportune time to produce the silver chain with the locket. "Fallow, Fidelity, I know that I cannot bring back your daughter but she would have wanted you to have this." He places the locket and chain in Fidelity's hands. She breaks down.

Fallow now knows what he has to do. "Take him to the stable and tie him to the hitching post. I'll be along directly after I fetch the Holy Book."

They do as he says and then Fallow enters the stable. Meecham is busy pounding a horseshoe into shape. "Meecham, hand me the bullwhip and be sure to close the stable door behind you."

Edge twists and turns at the hitching post as his hands are tied snuggly to the iron ring. Fallow unbuttons his long black coat places it and the hat on a bale of hay. He then rolls up the sleeves of the white shirt. He places the Bible next to the clothes and opens it. He then takes the bullwhip and uncoils it in his hands. He snaps his wrist and the bullwhip snaps sharply in the air.

It gets Edge's attention. "You don't have to do this," he

pleads. "Let me go and I'll pay you whatever you want, just say the word and it's yours."

Fallow steps up to Edge and places his lips next to the trapper's ear. "Can you give me back my daughter that you savagely raped and killed? I think not."

"I am sorry. It was the devil in me that caused it to happen."

Fallow steps away, paces off a few steps, and commences to lay the bullwhip. He commences to quote passages from the bible. "*Vengeance is mine sayeth the Lord, Romans twelve through nineteen.*" The snap of the bullwhip cuts away the shirt and it slashes Edge's back. He cries out in pain.

"*Get behind me Satan, Matthew sixteen.*" Fallow increases the tempo with the flick of his wrist. The bullwhip nicks Edge's earlobes and his neck. "*Before the cock crows three times, you will disown me, Matthew twenty six to thirty six.*"

Edge's wails spook the horses. They kick up a fuss, bucking about in the wooden stalls. Fallow wipes away the sweat he has worked up with his shirt sleeve. He closes the Bible and in so doing he feels a strange presence inside the stable. It is the spirit of Mabel. He can feel her hand on his as he grips the bullwhip. He commences the whipping. "*Amazing grace how sweet the sound that saved a wretch like me I once was lost but now I'm found was blind but now I see.*" Edge drops his head to his chest, his knees have buckled and his ankles bow out.

"Forty lashes that is sufficient for the crime you have committed. Another man would have killed you for what you have done and rightfully so." Fallow curls up the bullwhip, then hangs it on the hook. He then rolls down the shirtsleeves, collects his hat, long black coat, and the Bible.

Edge falls to his knees, still tied to the hitching post. His shirt is in tatters, the deep welts from the whipping oozing blood. Fallow opens the stable door and Flea darts in. The dog circles around Edge, smelling the fresh blood. Edge opens his eyes, "Get out of here, you mangy mutt!" Flea raises its hind leg and pees on Edge's back. He yells and curses at the dog. When Flea is done, he kicks up dirt with his back legs that stick on the open wounds of Edge's back.

24

CASSIDY CONVINCES HIS FATHER to escort him to where he thinks the Spanish treasure is buried. They set out accompanied with Flea in hopes of returning richer than when they departed.

Likewise Mohe and Hialeah have set out to return to the Cherokee camp.

Walker negotiates the purchase of a wagon and a pair of mules so that he can transport Duncan Edge back to Chicago. The trapper is in no condition to ride a mount. When they pass through the gates some of the men spit at Edge. "Good riddance to a vile and evil man," Bonnie Haggard stating her displeasure.

~ ~ ~

The Cherokee led by Chief Koatohee surround the colony. It is mid-afternoon, a bright and crisp autumn day. The schoolhouse bell is ringing to alert all of the impending doom. "To arms, to arms, the enemy is at the gates," the sentry shouts as he scurries hither and yon.

The attack is well staged as the chief has strategically placed the braves who are armed with bows and arrows. Their targets are within striking distance.

Fallow orders that all of the lamp oils be poured on the fortified fieldstone walls and when he deems it is necessary to ignite it, creating a fiery shield that will protect them from the Indians. "Men, man your weapons. There will be no quarter nor surrender. Women take shelter along with your children. Do not fear for God will send down his angels to protect us. This is the New Jerusalem and we shall not perish!" Fallow's words echo throughout the hub of activity.

No sooner were his words spoken than the sky was

filled with arrows from all directions, raining down on them like streaks of lightning. It took everyone by surprise as several of the arrows found the intended targets, inflicting wounds to men, women, and children indiscriminatingly. The cries of pain and anguish were apparent as the wounded are hastily moved into the church where a triage was supervised by Bonnie Haggard and Candice Lynch. Quickly and expeditiously, the wounded arrive and now volley after volley of muskets respond, filling the air with a fog of war. The cries of war whoops from the Cherokee send chills up the spines and goosebumps down the arms, scaring the bejesus out of the colonists.

The ammunition has almost been exhausted and so their last resort is to ignite the oils, which will provide a last line of defense. Once the oils are lit, there will be no chance to escape. The perimeter around the compound is completely engulfed making it virtually impossible to see beyond the tall tongues of the flickering flames.

Fallow gathers everyone into the town square and directs them to kneel down and begin to pray. The wounded are tended but the fresh water is quickly being depleted from the well.

Then the unexpected happens; Abagail Broom, Hester Adams, along with Rebecca Lynch dressed in their red bonnets and clutching the pushpin dolls advance shoulder-to-shoulder to the main gate, which is now totally engulfed in flames. Fallow orders a group of young men to stop the teenage girls, but they are unable to move. The pushpins are being poked into the dolls inflicting pain into the young men's arms and legs. The girls are undeterred as they proceed into the raging inferno. Mothers shield the eyes of their children so that they cannot see. But the girls are not harmed, their clothes are not singed as they emerge outside the burning ring of fire. Waiting to greet them is none other than Ida Mae with her arms open wide.

Upon seeing this Chief Koatohee bows down to give them honor and so do all of the Cherokee war party.

Then the black leper leads the teenage girls into the woods. Truly a miracle has taken place that shall not soon be forgotten.

25

CASSIDY'S HYPOTHESIS of where the Spanish buried treasure could be found was right on the money. The remnants of a wooden fort built by the conquistadors, only to be burned down to the ground by the Guitaris in retribution, are in evidence. At the foot of Meigs Falls, located on the southern bank of the Little River, the stockade walls stand in place as if they are wooden sentries, the sole survivors of what transpired centuries ago.

Flea has detected a strong scent permeating out of the ground. The dog digs at the dirt with its front paws, the sand and pebbles pepper-spray Cassidy and Brennon who are standing in the line of fire.

"I wonder what has drawn Flea's curiosity, son."

"I sure hope it's the buried treasure, Pa."

It doesn't take Flea long to unearth what has been covered in this remote outpost. The slats of wood fastened with forged metal straps and nails come into view. Father and son drop to their knees and begin to remove the dirt using only their bare hands. They are giddy with delight as the heat from the noonday sun permeates throughout their clothes. Together they hold fast to the leather strap handles and hoist the chest from the earth. The contents of the chest are demanding to lift both mentally and physically.

Father and son have been waiting for this day ever since the initial letter was read. The wooden chest is secured with a rusty padlock. Cassidy dashes into the river to seek a heavy stone to break open the padlock. They take turns attempting to unlock the chest. At long last the stone does its job the padlock snaps open. Cassidy removes it from the metal clasp. They raise the top of the wooden chest to find an ornate banner of red white and gold emblazoned with the crucified Jesus Christ. It is shielding what has been stored inside the chest.

Brennon respectfully removes the banner to reveal the precious Spanish treasure. There are chalices encrusted with precious gems, doubloons of silver and gold, rings set with precious stones, a sparkling splendor that is reflected by the rays of the sun. As they remove the treasure, they find a leather pouch.

Cassidy unloosens the knotted cord to reveal its contents. A piece of brown burlap that was of the habit worn by Padre Santiago and strands of hair tied to a feather and a scroll. Could this be the reason why the chest was buried and not the gold and silver?

Brennon unrolls the scroll, noting that it is written in Spanish. He translates the message to Cassidy. *"I have sold my soul to the devil in trade for my love of the Indian maiden Oceeannalee. May God have mercy upon me, for I have strayed. The spirit is strong but the flesh is weak. Padre Phillipe Santiago."*

"So all of this treasure belonged to a Spanish priest, Pa?"

"I don't think so, but whoever buried this chest made sure to keep whatever took their life a secret, in the hope that it could never be found."

The sky suddenly turns dark as heavy clouds move in to obscure the sun. The wind picks up, blowing in from the north, causing ripples to form on the surface of the Little River. A strong stench of decaying flesh permeates the air. Cassidy and Brennon turn around to confront Ida Mae accompanied by Abagail, Hester, and Rebecca.

"I see you have found what is mine. Yes, after all these years I will reclaim what is rightfully mine, my precious."

"Yours, I think not! We found this fair and square, to the victor belongs the spoils!"

"Oh you foolish old man, do you know who you are dealing with? Do you not see these fair maidens who are under my spell? I could have killed your offspring in the cemetery when he found the initial letter hidden inside of the old hickory tree, but I decided to let him live. And you know why? Because I knew that he was the chosen one who was destined to discover the Spanish buried treasure chest. I was cursed so it had to be done, prearranged so that a child would bear the sign of the dead. That child, your son carries the sign, the severed tip of his finger that you removed to save his life. If not for you, we would not be here at this juncture today."

"I am not a religious man. I do believe in God. I only pray to him in times of need. But you are just some old black woman, a slave who has no claim to this Spanish treasure. Be gone with all of your foolish talk that you are entitled, as if you are in a long line of nobility to reclaim your title."

Ida Mae has heard enough. She opens the quilted bag and removes the pushpin doll. The girls do likewise, their hypnotic eyes firmly fixed upon her, in a trance awaiting further instructions. "Either you deliver to me what is rightfully mine or I shall inflict upon you and your son pain so intense that you will be pleading on your knees to be put to death." She holds a pin ready to push it into the dolls chest.

"Don't take my pa. Let him live to see another day."

"You are brave beyond your tender years. I dare say if not for you, your father would become a member of the lost colony at Dutch Bottoms."

"I do not understand what you are saying. We left them only a few days ago."

"A lot can happen between a setting sun and a rising moon." Then the leper replaces the pushpin doll back into the quilted bag. She takes the piece of the habit along with the strands of hair tied to the feather and rolls them up inside the scroll, tucks the items into the leather pouch, and deposits it into the quilted bag. Then in the blink of an eye she vanishes along with Abagail, Hester and Rebecca.

Brennon closes the chest, placing it back into the hole in the ground, and then reburies it.

"Pa, what are you doing? We're rich. Don't you want to tell the others, especially Ma?"

"No, I do not, for this treasure is cursed. It almost cost us our lives. Some things are meant not to be tampered with."

"Well, I know where it is, I'll destroy the map because I have no need for it anymore. But one day I'll return, sure as I know the back of my hand."

They return to Dutch Bottoms and discover not a soul is stirring including the missing livestock. Cassidy and Brennon venture into the homes where the tables are set for a meal to be shared. Inside the schoolbooks are opened for a lesson to be taught by the teacher. The pews in the church have hymnals ready for the faithful to sing the Lords praises. Also there are remnants of the wounded: bloody rags cover the stalls in the stable and throughout the barn.

Brennon and Cassidy follow Flea who enters the cemetery. Carved into the old hickory tree where Cassidy found the leather pouch are the letters OCEEANNALEE.

26

BRANCH WALKER IS HOLDING the reins loosely, letting the mules set the pace to pull the wagon. Duncan Edge is lying on his stomach because the whipping that Fallow gave to him is taking time to heal. They have travelled a few miles from Clingmans Dome and now are in the Ocanaluftee Valley.

A detachment of cavalry army soldiers ride up, heading in the opposite direction. They are led by Captain Drew Benteen and his top-kick, Sergeant Jefferson Armstrong. Walker pulls back on the reins and the mules slow down to a gentle stop. The horses shake their heads, the tails wagging side-to-side.

Benteen gestures a courtesy salute to Walker, who nods his head and spits out a mouthful of tobacco juice. "Where are you heading stranger?" Benteen asks Walker.

Edge stirs in the back of the wagon, trying to keep out of sight by covering his head with the mule blanket. "I'm on my way to Chicago to collect a reward that's a long time coming."

"What reward are you talking about, stranger?" Benteen asks.

"A man was shot some time ago and the killer was on the run from the law. I'm a bounty hunter and I got the individual in my custody. So if you don't mind, Captain, I'll be on my way."

Armstrong coaxes his horse to the back of the wagon where he observes Edge squirming about under the cover. The sergeant bends down from his saddle and yanks the cover from Edge. Edge hides his face with his hands. "Hey, Captain, take a look at what I found," Armstrong informs

Benteen.

The captain nudges his horse to where Armstrong is. "Well I be, if it isn't Private First Class Edge," Benteen exclaims.

Walker turns around in the seat to face the soldiers. "You know this man?" Walker asks them.

"Hell yeah, he has been away without leave for quite a spell. We knew sooner or later that he'd cross our path," Armstrong replies.

"Well, if you want him, you'll have to accompany me to Chicago, then after I get my reward, he's all yours."

"That's not going to happen, stranger. The government has jurisdiction over any outstanding warrants. Edge will be taken into custody and will be dealt with accordingly under the army regulations."

The rest of the detachment climb into the wagon and place Edge under military arrest. Edge is in no shape to ride a horse, his back still bearing the scars from the bullwhip.

"Who did this to you, soldier," Benteen asks him.

"I was whipped by Fallow Crowder for a crime I did not commit."

Benteen looks at Walker. "Is that accurate, stranger, what he is telling us?"

"He's lying through his teeth. He killed that man's daughter, then placed the blame on an Indian brave. But I saw through his veil of lies, just like I know that he killed a man back in Chicago."

Edge glares at Walker. "Don't believe him, Captain. All of what he's telling you is made up. I might be a deserter, but I'm not a cold-blooded killer."

Walker knows that he will have to hand Edge over or else there will be trouble and the outcome will not end well. He is outnumbered and outgunned. "Take him, Captain. Whatever he is in store for, make it count."

"Private First Class Edge, I place you under arrest. You

are a deserter who will be facing hard time. I will make sure that you will be placed in the stockade until you are well enough to break rocks in the scorching sun."

Walker remains silent as Edge is moved from the wagon to the ground.

"Sergeant, move out the men. Stranger, I owe you a debt of gratitude," Benteen bids Walker a farewell.

Walker watches them as they slowly ride away with Edge walking, tied to a rope. Walker snaps the reins and the mules respond. The trip back home will take some time and Walker has second thoughts about handing Edge over to the soldiers. What if they weren't soldiers but a band of outlaws in disguise? What if they were out to help Edge get away? What if they'll take him back to Chicago and cash in on the reward?

Walker spends the night out under the stars and the next morning breaks camp and heads for his cabin.

~ ~ ~

Brennon and Cassidy are devastated by what they saw at Dutch Bottoms. Where could Bonnie and the rest of the Amish be? How can an entire colony all of a sudden disappear? If anyone had the answer it would have to be Ida Mae.

Brennon and Cassidy come upon Walker's cabin, expecting to find him there. The cabin is empty so the father and son make themselves at home. Brennon lights a fire while Cassidy tries to catch fish for them to fry.

Walker notices white puffs of smoke rising from the chimney of the cabin. "I wonder who is squatting in my home. I'll fix a whipping on them, by golly."

Cassidy sees Walker on the wagon and waves to him. He runs to the cabin holding the fish that he just caught. "Hey, Pa, come quick. It is Mister Walker."

Brennon comes out of the cabin to greet him. The trapper is in no mood for pleasantries; he is still grumpy from losing out on the reward. "How was Chicago? Did you collect the reward in return for bringing in Edge?" Brennon asks.

Walker pulls back on the reins, then ties them to the handbrake. He spits out the tobacco juice and climbs down from the wagons seat. "Nope, plans didn't work out the way I expected. I met up with the army, who took him into custody. It turns out that Edge was a deserter."

"A deserter, huh? Who would have figured that? Say, let's have us some fresh fish that my boy just caught from the river. I hope you aren't sore about us partaking of your hospitality, but you see there's nothing for us to go back to."

Walker looks at Brennon with puzzlement, "Why is that?"

Cassidy fills him in on what happened at Dutch Bottoms.

"That is the craziest thing I have ever heard of, and you say there isn't a clue as to where they might have gone?"

"The only logical reason would be that the Cherokee came and took them away, to where I have no idea."

"Maybe they have them at the camp where I was taken. I know where that is. Do you want me to show you? It isn't that far."

They scale the fish and fill their bellies. Walker unhitches the mules from the wagon and leads them to the creek to drink.

Brennon joins him by the creek. "Say, Walker, I was just thinking about those soldiers you met up with."

"Go ahead, I'm listening."

"Which direction were they heading?"

"Well, let me think. I was heading east so I guess they were heading west."

"Huh, west you say? So they were traveling this a way."

"I reckon, why do you ask?" "

Well the only reason for the army to travel here is to

check on the Indians or to visit Dutch Bottoms. I mean it doesn't make any other sense what their intentions could be."

"I know darn well that Dutch Bottoms wouldn't be their destination and if they were scouting for the Indians, they would be sorry, for sure."

Walker motions to Cassidy who is playing with Flea on the cabin porch. "I think we need to take a visit to the Cherokee camp and find out what's what. Can we get there in a day's walk?"

"I think so. If we follow the creek up north, we can cut off a couple of miles from the trip."

They head out the next day at first light and follow Cassidy's lead. When they are within sight of the Cherokee camp, Walker and Brennon raise their rifles high above their heads to show the Indians that they come in peace. There are several braves and squaw at the creek bed who quickly surround them.

Adahy and Tsiyi ride up on their ponies and dismount. They recognize Cassidy, who greets them with a hug. The braves and the squaws allow them to pass into the middle of the camp where they meet Chief Koatohee and Chief Oconostota.

"We come in peace. We mean you no harm," Walker tells them.

The two chiefs spot Cassidy and they are happy to see him again. "Look, it is little Sure Shot," Chief Koatohee comments. He gestures to them to enter the council lodge, where they can have some privacy. Inside the lodge, they pass around the peace pipe.

Walker and Brennon convey to the chiefs why they are here and ask about the Amish colony. Chief Koatohee replies to them, "There were three white girls who walked through fire that surrounded the village. We saw that as a sign so we left. Now you say that all of the whites are missing?"

"Yes, chief, and we wanted to alert you that the army is scouting for your camp. We believe that they will bring nothing but trouble to your people," Walker warns.

"My daughter Hialeah has told me much about you, Snow Hair. She has opened my eyes that have been asleep for many moons. Now I understand what she says. Not all white men are our enemies."

"Thank you Chief. I respect the Cherokee; that is why we came here to warn you. Is Hialeah in the camp? I miss her and also Mohe."

"They are in the camp. I will send for them."

They are invited to spend the night and are hosted with a feast in their honor. Walker sits near Hialeah, Chief Koatohee making it a point to be seated between them.

However Oconostota is less tolerant of the guests. "We have never been accepted in the white man's lodge but here they are in ours. The Indians see what is near to them and accept what it is, but the white man is not satisfied. He looks to the far horizon and takes what is not his. As long as we have our differences there shall never be peace between us." Chief Oconostota walks out of the council lodge after saying his peace.

"He is wrong, Father. I have been a guest in Snow Hair's house and never felt afraid. We must find a way to build a bridge to take down the walls that divide us."

Brennon is feeling a deep loss for his wife Bonnie. What has been bottled up, now is evident as he cannot control his emotions. It is rare for an Indian male to cry in the presence of others. Cassidy hugs him in a show of love for his father.

"They have been through a lot," Walker comments stating the obvious. "If the soldiers would come into your camp and take away your loved ones, you would feel the same as them."

"If the soldiers would ever try to set foot on our land,

we would fight them to the death," Mohe declares as he draws his hunting knife.

"Enough talk about war or hatred. We should be celebrating the common ground between us. The night is still young and the stars have given us much light for us to shine. Let us be happy for all that the Great Spirit has given to us."

"My daughter is wise, much wiser than I am. Our guests are welcome to stay until the morning sun rises in the sky."

Fog hung heavily to the earth the next morning as Walker, Cassidy, and Brennon depart the camp. They dare not disturb their hosts for fear of a reprisal. They are heading back to Walker's place when they realize that someone is shadowing them. Flea barks at the stirring inside the thick brush. It is Mohe and Hialeah, who have decided to accompany them just in case Chief Oconostota may have sent his braves to do harm.

As the fog dissipates, the sun gives way and a warm breeze wafts through the lofty tall timbers. Brennon and Cassidy have their minds set not to return with Walker, but to pursue a new path to the south. There at the summit of Clingmans Dome, they will be able to view from on high the scenery that surrounds them. Hopefully, wherever the Amish might be, it will be apparent from the vantage point.

Walker and Hialeah arrive back at his place, where they waste no time in making love. She is so beautiful he cannot believe his eyes; and he is everything she has ever wanted in a man: strong, kind hearted, and honest as the day is long. They slip off their clothes and make deep passionate love on the bearskin rugs that grace the dirt floor.

Later, Walker pulls on his britches and wades into the Molasses Creek. He is holding a woven basket just below the surface and waits for a catch. Hialeah stands at the open door wrapped in a rug while she brushes her long black hair and watches her lover. The sunbeams sparkle on the tiny rivulets as Walker tiptoes over the protruding rocks at the bottom of the creek. A school of fish, swim up the creek avoiding the basket but now Walker's attention is being diverted to a shiny object between his toes. A stone glimmers. Walker bends down and extracts it from the sand. He holds it up to his eyes, drops the basket into the water, then shouts with delight. "Gold, there's gold in the water, and it's mine all mine!" He sloshes through the shallow water, giddy as a child skipping in a muddy puddle.

Hialeah can't help but wonder what has gotten into him that is making her man so excited. "I'm rich, I mean we're rich, and is all because of this," Walker showing her the golden nugget.

"Rich, what is rich? I do not know what that means."

Walker lets out a hearty laugh. "Rich means that you buy things, pretty things that cost a fortune, and it is all thanks to this little piece of gold."

"That yellow rock is just that, nothing more."

"Hialeah, my dear, don't you see? Whatever you want, you can have it."

"But I have everything I need. What more do I want?"

He tries to explain to her in simple words how the white man's way of living is so different than the Indians. "Let's say I have something that you want. Well, I would set a price and you would pay me in exchange."

"Oh, I see like a trade. You give me a blanket and I give you a pony?"

"Exactly, Hialeah. Now you're catching on to what I've been trying to tell you. I need to stake my claim for the rights to pan the creek for gold so that nobody can cheat me out of my fortune. I will have to go back east to do so. Do you want to come along?"

She ponders his invitation for a few moments. "It would be better for me to stay. You go and I'll wait for your return. The yellow rocks will be safeguarded by the Great Spirit."

She turns her back to him and lets the bearskin fall from her body.

"Aw what the hell, maybe you're right. I got everything here that gold just can't buy."

~ ~ ~

Leading a battalion of cavalry is General Lucius Hannibal. He is one of the youngest cadets to have graduated from West Point. Now he is in charge of moving the Cherokee from their land to a reservation in Oklahoma. He summons Captain Benteen to ride along side of him. "Captain, take a few of the scouts and head to that high cliff," he points to Clingmans Dome, "then report back to me what you find."

"Yes sir," Benteen replies as he smartly salutes his superior officer. He then turns his horse and rides away with Sergeant Armstrong and two Indian scouts of the Oconaluftee tribe.

From the summit of Clingmans Dome, Mohe, Cassidy, and Brennon survey what lies below. Brennon shields his eyes from the sun. Forlornly, he surmises, "Where could the god-fearing Amish be? It is as if the ground opened and sucked the life out of them. Or has the *Rapture* occurred and they were carried away up to heaven?"

Mohe spots the long lines of the army advancing from the north into the valley below. He points to their position. "Look, there are many horse soldiers coming this way. I must alert my people before it is too late."

As they are descending Clingmans Dome, the army scouting party ride up. Mohe draws his bow, Brennon cocks the trigger on his rifle, and Cassidy loads his slingshot.

The soldiers surround them on their horses. "Well, look what we got here -- an Indian, an old coot, and a snot-nose brat," Armstrong comments as he pulls tight on the reins.

"Sergeant I order you to place them under arrest."

Brennon is incredulous." But we haven't committed

any crime. We shall stand our ground. I would suggest that you ride back to where you came from."

Armstrong's free hand grips the handle of his pistol still in the holster. The two scouts pace their horses back and forth while Benteen looks over his shoulder at the advancing command of cavalry. If he captures Mohe, Brennon, and the boy without firing a shot, it will add another citation for advancement.

All of a sudden Flea scampers down the rise and starts barking, which spooks the horses. Armstrong pulls out his pistol and then Cassidy releases his slingshot. The small rock hits Armstrong's horse in the side, then one of the Indian scouts takes aim with his rifle to fire but Mohe's arrow takes flight, hitting the Indian scout dead-center in his chest. The scout falls from his saddle fatally wounded.

Benteen draws his pistol and fires at Mohe, but misses, the bullet piercing Brennon in his heart. He drops the rifle and collapses. Cassidy runs to his father and cradles his head. "Pa, are you alright?" Brennon looks up at his son and coughs up a mouthful of blood. "Pa, don't you die on me, you hear me? I can't lose you, who will look after me. I'll be all alone. Pa, can you see me? God, please don't take him from me, not now."

Mohe decides to make a run for it, as Armstrong and the other scout pursue him across the valley. Mohe is nearly shot by the bullets being fired from his pursuers. Where the edge of the timberline converges, Mohe is able to zigzag out of harm's way. Once he is in the woods he runs as fast as his feet will carry him back to the camp.

Once he arrives, he alerts the Cherokee of the advancing army.

Benteen aims his pistol at Cassidy, but Flea jumps up and bites him on his forearm and will not let go. Cassidy lays his father down, then reloads his slingshot takes aim and hits Benteen right between the eyes. Flea lets go of his arm and the captain holding on to the horse's mane, gallops away.

"Pa, remember the Spanish buried treasure we found? We have to dig it back up and find ma." But Brennon has died. Cassidy drags his father's lifeless body to a secluded spot where he cannot be seen and buries the body beneath a pile of rocks. He waits until he thinks it is safe to make a move.

Benteen joins up with Armstrong and the scout in the middle of the valley. There is a nasty gash of the bridge of Benteen's nose, and the bite from Flea has him clutching his arm. "Are you alright captain," Armstrong asks.

"Yes, did you kill the Indian?"

"Nope, he eluded us into the woods. What about the scout captain? Is he dead?"

"I'm afraid so, that renegade now has a price of his head and I want to see him brought to justice."

"Begging your pardon, sir, but we must be close to the Cherokee camp," the scout comments. "Come now, let us not delay and report to General Hannibal what has happened."

Cassidy and Flea make their way back to Walker's place to alert them. "Where is your pa, son," Walker asks.

"The soldiers shot him. He was killed in cold blood. That isn't right. Now I'm all alone, an orphan and no place to call my home." No sooner has Cassidy spoken when the sound of cannon fire explodes in the air, the reverberations can be felt from the ground.

Hialeah wants to return to the Cherokee camp but Walker refuses to let her leave. "It is too dangerous. Stay here where you will be safe. Cassidy, you look after her until I get back. If I am not back before sun up, go to the Demons Anvil and hide out in the cave."

Walker grabs his rifle, powder horn, and his hunting knife, but leaves behind the two pistols. "Use them if you have to," he says as he kisses Hialeah goodbye and pats the boy's head.

~ ~ ~

The Cherokee have never had to deal with an adversary that possessed in their arsenal cannons that could be fired from a mile away. But what the Cherokee has in their favor is the terrain. They knew that if an enemy would attack, they had to tackle the dense woods. The cannons were not equipped to maneuver in tight locations, the logistics not feasible.

Chiefs Oconostota and Koatohee divide the braves into two distinct groups -- one would be sent to slow down the onslaught and the other would defend the camp at all costs. Oconostota's braves roll heavy stones on the trail to impede Hannibal's advancing troops. Then they disperse and lie in waiting, hiding behind rocks, trees, and the dense brush. The army has no idea that by using guerilla warfare the Cherokee for the time have the upper hand.

General Hannibal has seen his share of battles. He lost an eye fighting in the French and Indian Wars at Fort Ticonderoga. He draws up a strategic plan where the cavalry will be best suited to hem in the camp. By flanking the camp, there will be far less casualties and the cannons can be used to the optimum potential.

Mohe, Aday, and Tsiyi are assigned to stay in the camp with the elders, the women, and children. These brave warriors feel that they should be with Oconostota, but they will do whatever necessary to save the weak from being killed by the soldier's bullets and bayonets. "This is the day the Great Spirit has made for us to vanquish our enemies or to die trying."

Wise Sparrow heeds Chief Koatohee's impassioned words outside her lodge. "Do not worry, old woman, I will not let the horse soldiers take one strand of hair from your head," Mohe assures her.

It doesn't take long before the bitter enemies commence to killing one another. Back and forth the tides change -- the army advances, then the Indians counter attack.

Hannibal presses his men not to cede any ground. "Bugler, sound the charge!"

The defenders of the camp are now being attacked from the flanks. With the soldiers shooting at will, many of the women and children are killed. Several of the lodges are set on fire and whoever are inside are shot once they attempt to flee from the flames.

Two soldiers enter Wise Sparrow's lodge where Mohe fights them to the death, his tomahawk and knife smash and slash at the soldiers.

Chief Koatohee realizes that the tribe will be slaughtered if he does not surrender the camp. He pleads with the soldiers to stop shooting but instead he is bayonetted for his effort. Adahy stabs the soldier in his back and he falls down dead. The ensuing soldiers will not cease fire until the order has been given.

Hannibal orders the cannoneers to commence firing. The salvo of the cannonballs hail down on the camp and the lodges are blown to bits. Needless to say that many Cherokee and soldiers are killed or gravely wounded. Mohe, Adahy, and Tsiyi have to make a decision to fight to the death or flee. They agree that they shall not surrender their weapons but instead make a hasty retreat into the woods.

Chief Oconostota concedes defeat to General Hannibal as the soldiers round up the braves and the rest of the tribe. Captain Benteen is still licking his wounds, seated in the saddle as the Cherokee prisoners are paraded past him. Sergeant Armstrong rides up and comments, "I don't see that Indian that killed our scout captain."

"Neither do I. Maybe he was killed back in the camp."

"No sir, I had my men check in case any of the Injuns

were playing dead."

"Well, check again, Sergeant. Bayonet everybody to make it official."

"Will do, Captain." Armstrong kicks his heels into the horse's flanks and rides off.

Walker's path crosses with Mohe, Adahy, and Tsiyi. They are not pleased to see him. Tsiyi draws his bow but Mohe grabs for it, saving Walker's life. "The horse soldiers have killed many of the tribe. You Snow Hair has been an enemy and a friend. What are you now to us?" Mohe asks him.

"I am your friend. Come with me to where you will be safe."

Adahy has his doubts. "How do we know that you aren't going to hand us over to the horse soldiers, Snow Hair?"

"You don't" he opens his shirt to show the scar from the arrow. "I could have taken you out before you ever saw me. Look, we don't have much time before the soldiers figure out that Mohe hasn't been killed or captured. Follow the trail to the creek where my place is, there you will find Hialeah and the boy." The braves must take Walker's advice while he makes his way to the army and sends them off in the wrong direction.

~ ~ ~

Hannibal is informed by Benteen that a few of the braves have eluded them, so he orders a squad to track them down. The rest of the battalion will proceed to move the Cherokee to Oklahoma.

Walker volunteers to aid in tracking the braves, which Hannibal is thankful for. But Benteen informs the general that it was Walker who was taking Edge to Chicago and claiming the bounty for a murder. "I see," the general ponders. "So what should we do, Captain?"

"If I were you, General, I would place my bets on the Indian scout. He knows the territory better than anyone."

Walker can't help but overhear their conversation. "Have it your way. I am only telling you what I saw, but if you want to track them based on an Injun I won't stand in your way." Walker makes it a point not to leave the way he came, so he takes the long way back to his place.

"General, what should we do with the dead?" Sergeant Armstrong asks.

"Bury the brave soldiers sorry to say that were lost from friendly fire. But as in any battle collateral damage never outweighs the victory." After the soldiers are buried in a common grave, Taps was played by the bugler. Just as the sun was setting, the trek to Oklahoma began.

For the time being, the Cherokee braves were safe at Walker's place, but an air of uncertainty was apparent. They knew that a scouting party would arrive and if the braves were found it would be a bloodbath. A new hideout had to be found before the winter snows would fall. Adahy observes a white owl flying over the creek. He calls to the braves, "It is a bad sign of a cold weather to come."

No truer were the words that he spoke. On the trail to Oklahoma, a cold northern gale pushed a massive and treacherous storm. It snowed relentlessly for more than fifteen hours as the temperature plummeted to a minus 21°. Over the next few days, the temperature continued to dip until it reached an incredible 44° below zero. For as far as the eyes could see, everything was white, not a spot of the earth visible. The storm lasted nine days without letting up. It took its toll on the cattle that was to feed the army and the Cherokee. The elderly and the children were the most vulnerable to the weather.

It was just a matter of time before Wise Sparrow walked her last steps. She fell into a snow bank. A soldier ordered her to get up. There was no response from her. Again the soldier ordered her to get up.

"You're too easy on her. Let me show you how it's done.

Hey, old woman, if you don't get up, I'll make you, so what's it going to be?"

Captain Benteen rides up to assess the situation. "What seems to be the problem, private?"

"There is no problem, Captain. I have it all under control."

"Very well, carry on, soldier."

"See what you've done? I am in big trouble with the captain. Get up and move on." There is no reply from her. The private kicks her, then notices that she is not moving. Just to make sure that she is indeed dead, he shoves the bayonet into her side and then rolls her over.

Another soldier comments, "You know something, Edge, she could have passed for a white woman, fancy that."

By the time the Cherokee finally arrive at the destination, more than 4,000 of the 17,000 died on the trail from disease, starvation, and the brutal weather. The reservation -- for the lack of a better word -- is nothing more than a prison.

General Hannibal makes it a point to meet with Chief Oconostota before he signs off on the exchange of the Cherokee to the designated officer in charge. "You now have a new home, Chief. Get used to the surroundings. Here you will be free to live out your life in peace."

"Why did you come to our camp, General? Why didn't you just let us be?"

"You were in the way. I had orders to move you. It came from President Andrew Jackson."

"The Great White Father in Washington has nothing to fear from us. We are a peaceful people. We want nothing but to be left alone."

Hannibal points to the patch over his eye. "I know from experience all about the Indians, Chief. I lost my eye from a savage that was involved with attacking settlers, killing and scalping defenseless women and children in their beds."

"You did the same, General, attacking my camp. I lost many members of the tribe. There are families who lost mothers, fathers, grandparents, and their children. Then you forced upon us to walk through the dead of winter, knowing that many would never complete the journey."

"Chief, your ways are of the past. America is growing; it needs to progress in order to meet the demands of its people."

"So you take our land, our way of life, and expect us to be pleased with your decision? We are like the buffalo. This land is ours has been for many moons. If you think that by moving us to a reservation that peace will come to the white man you are mistaken. No, General, for as long as there are brave warriors out there living free and defying you, they will follow the war path."

"If you are speaking about the renegades that got away, Chief, they will be hunted down and ultimately will be captured. It is only just a matter of time."

"We will assemble a meeting, then we will honor the Great Spirit and praise all who died bravely fighting the white man. We shall partake in the Ghost Dance and will not be silent."

"Dance to your hearts content, Chief, but know this: you shall never leave the reservation."

As Hannibal mounts his horse, Chief Oconostota looks up at him, then grabs the reins. "One day America will be attacked by enemies from a far-off land. They will speak in a different tongue and bring many fighters who will not be afraid to die for their cause. Cities will burn, many people will die. Then you will know what the Cherokee and all the tribes went through. This land is meant to be shared, no one owns it. We are only the caretakers."

~ ~ ~

The heavy snows not only fell west of the Smokies but throughout the Great Plains and the valleys. Walker's cabin is covered in heavy snow at least four feet or more with drifts nearly ten feet. The Oconaluftee scouts have been searching for Mohe, Adahy, and Tsiyi for several weeks.

When they arrive at Walker's place, he opens the door to the cabin with the rifle in his hands. The scouts want to know about the braves. "I don't know where they are. For all I know they could be anywhere."

Standing behind Walker is Hialeah and Cassidy. The scouts want to know about them. "She's my wife and he's my son. Now if you don't get off my land, I just might want to shoot one of you dead, now get."

The scouts take their time to leave his place.

The Cherokee braves have been on the move ever since they left Walker's cabin. Even though the heavy snows made it next to impossible to ride a horse, the braves had the tenacity. They wrapped deerskin around the horse's hooves so that they could not be tracked. They stayed for a spell at Demons Anvil, then headed north to Grotto Falls where they were able to catch fresh fish. Once spring came, then the scouts would join up with a fresh squad of cavalry soldiers who would hunt them down. They were eventually captured at Moose Creek Falls, but not without a fight. They were shipped to the reservation in Oklahoma, where the Cherokee were happy to see them.

Captain Benteen left specific orders to be notified when Mohe was captured. When the officer of the reservation asked who was Mohe, both Adahy and Tsiyi replied, "I am Mohe."

They were placed in the stockade until the day would come when they would be executed by a firing squad. On a Sunday morning, they were led out of their cells and marched out into the prison yard their arms and legs shackled in chains. Mohe, Adahy, and Tsiyi are asked if they wanted a blindfold for their eyes so they would not have to see the executioner's faces. All of them refused. The firing squad marched out in single file and took up their positions, then waited for the order to fire their rifles. It was over in a matter of seconds. In a twist of fate Duncan Edge fired the fatal bullet that took Mohe's life.

Mohe, Adahy, and Tsiyi would forever be remembered by the Cherokee as heroes.

~ ~ ~

Cassidy decides that he will leave Walker and Hialeah to seek out the whereabouts of his mother and the rest of the missing colony. Hialeah wants him to stay. "Don't go, Cassidy. Here you are safe. We can be a family. Snow Hair and I love you as if you were our son."

However, Cassidy has his mind set and nothing that they say will convince him. "I'll be all right. I have Flea to keep me company. I have my trusty slingshot in my back pocket so I am ready for whatever may come my way." He kisses Hialeah farewell and hugs Walker in a tight embrace.

Hialeah cries as they watch him walk away. "Cassidy, don't go, come back" she calls to him.

Cassidy turns his head and smiles at her. "Who knows, maybe I'll find me the secret of the Spanish buried treasure and I'll be rich."

To which Walker replies, "Whatever you find you'll have to share it with us."

"I'll never divulge its location, after all a secret is a secret forever. That's what my pa told me and I'm not about to break the bond. C'mon, Flea, let's rustle up some jackrabbits and maybe if we're lucky we'll catch us a bullfrog. Who knows what is waiting for us down the untraveled road yonder?"

CONCLUSION

WALKER AND HIALEAH remain at Molasses Creek and raise a family. Cassidy never reveals where the Spanish buried treasure can be found. But the story does not end there.

In 1828 gold was discovered in the Great Smoky Mountains. President Jackson enacted the Removal Act in 1830 which forced 14,000 Cherokee to relocate to Oklahoma. The six-month journey took its toll, 4,000 dying during the arduous trek better known as the Trail of Tears.

A group of Cherokee refused to leave their land so the Oconaluftee reluctantly assisted the U.S. Army to round them up. The leader was considered a hero to the Cherokee, but was wanted as a fugitive to the government. On behalf of the Indians, lawyers took their case to court and sued the government of taking their land. These suits would eventually be decided in Washington by the Supreme Court.

The nine judges were evenly divided, those opposed to granting the Indians land stated that is it the Indians' intent to impede upon the progress of the country. In order for America to prosper, it needs to expand its horizons westward, and if in so doing, the government deems that the indigenous people need to be relocated, then so be it.

The judges who were in favor of the Indians being granted land also let it be known that if the government has the power to relocate the native peoples to a designated area, then every American will come to realize that at any given time they also could forfeit their land.

What broke the deadlock among the nine judges was some sage advice that time generally reveals down the road what a falsehood has to hide. So then, these Cherokee now called the Eastern Band were allowed to claim some of their lands in Western North Carolina in the 1870's. It took almost 20 years before 56,000 acres were set aside named the Qualla Indian Reservation.

The Walker clan and eventually the Haggards became farmers raising corn and tobacco. During the Great Depression many sawmills were shut down. Most of the farmers had a tough time selling their crops and they turned to moonshining. The struggle to survive during the Depression took its toll but was greatly reduced when the Civilian Conservation Corps established a camp. Trails were constructed for the newly created Great Smoky Mountains National Park. This huge project and the TVA began working on the Douglas Dam, which would provide electricity to Tennessee.

The Walkers and the Haggards had one of the two largest stills east of the Missouri River Then just like the Cherokee and the other tribes, the government decided to remove the farmers so that the Great Smoky Mountains Park could open to the public. The government gave the farmers a fair price for their land but some were reluctant to sell. Old friends and acquaintances -- many had lived there for generations -- like the Walkers and the Haggards had to find a new home and another way to live. To this day among the many fields of crops that the farmers plow, just below the surface is the Spanish buried treasure.

The Appalachian Trail meanders from Georgia to Maine passing through the Great Smoky Mountains range. There have been hikers who wish to remain anonymous for fear they will be ridiculed. Some nonbelievers scoff and commented that too much imbibing of white lightning (the clear liquid better known as moonshine) will make one see and hear things that don't exist. But if you may one day be hiking along the Appalachian Trail in or around the vicinity of Gatlinburg and Pigeon Forge, be prepared for the unexpected. Close encounters occur when the fog is dense early in morning, although there have been several sightings when the moon at night is full. Hikers have sensed a distinct strong odor of decaying flesh lingering in the air. Others have seen bright colors of red moving among the thick tree branches. There also has on occasion been a rustling in the bushes, then the sound of a barking dog. Could it be Ida Mae and the witches Abagail Broom, Hester Adams, and Rebecca Lynch being pursued by Cassidy's dog Flea?

By the way, the Spanish buried treasure has never been found, although the remnants of a Spanish fort are actively being excavated in North Carolina. At the site, pottery, lead nails, iron wire, and chain mail have been discovered. Fact is crazier than fiction. For you see, the soil nurtures every living thing. And in the scheme of the grand design we are all connected with deep seeded roots holding fast to our destiny.

Thank you for reading.
Please review this book. Reviews help others find
Absolutely Amazing eBooks and inspire us to keep
providing these marvelous tales.

If you would like to be put on our email list to receive
updates on new releases, contests, and promotions, please
go to AbsolutelyAmazingEbooks.com and sign up.

About the Author

James R. Fox received an Associate Liberal Arts degree from Queens Borough Community College. Now retired, he devotes his attention to writing, music, photography, traveling, and reading. Among his publications are *The Wake*, *Wisdom of Wishes*, *Christmas Eve*, and *The Map of the Carpenter*. His "Key West" was selected for inclusion in *The 2013 Robert Frost International Poetry and Haiku Contest* anthology.

www.ingramcontent.com/pod-product-compliance
Lightning Source LLC
Chambersburg PA
CBHW050404030726
47503CB00006B/2017